KIDNAPPED BY THE DRAGON

MANDY ROSKO

Cover art by Melody Simmons of Book Covers Cre8tive

Edited by Brieanna Robertson, Beth Fawcett, and Jessica Ripley

Published by Eighth Ripple Press

Print ISBN: 978-1-9990270-6-3

Ebook ISBN: 978-1-9990270-7-0

CONTENTS

DEDICATION

This book is dedicated to all of my patrons from 2019 over on Patreon! Thank you for your support! - Mandy

Nancy Mcdonald, Tami Gryder, Jessica Ripley, Nicole Henry, Barbara Burdette, Johanna Snodgrass, Andi Downs, Alisha Derr, Nicole Cook, Michelle Fortune, Teresa Ward, Sherry Smith, Angie Kyle, Melinda Miller, Leslie Gordon, Saleena Chamberlin, Ramona Cabrera, Dusty Weller, Terri Eaches.

Daria Donnelly, Kayla Reindl, Clare Parrott, Patricia Cassar, Sheryl Tegtmeyer, Lori Martin, Anne Rindfliesch, Stacy Ittersagen, Megan Mills, Christina Morgan, Monica Lynn Emery, Leanne Ede, Cassandra Hyden.

Anne Samson, Pauline Dixon, Rachelle Binkley, Rebekah Snyder, Michelle Chantler, Thomas Werner, Kaer Baer, Sharron Anthony, Roxanne Johnson, Rachel Morse, Karen, Marlene Eaton, Julie Spencer, Wendy Custer, Annette Alex, Shelia Deal, Carolyn Lown, Mellissa, Jill Micklich, Confused Child, Samalee Johnson, Sandy Folz, Janet Rodman, Jeanne Clark, David Friend.

Lizzy, Soshanahlila, Alexandra Smith, Virginia Robinson, Donna Hogel, Nanci Quinn, Janice Richmond, Stacey F, Barb Sands, Marcy Schwendiman, Charlotte Brincat, Sharon Manning-Lew, Teresa Albarran, Gerryann L., Denise Holder, Gail Powell, Rose Allen.

Opal Carew Lori Trask, Retiredhsmom, Maria T, Rachel Barckhaus, Laura Furuta, Angela Cowen, Diana Mason, Beth Wolfe, Toni Mcconnell, Valerie Cobb, Valerie Jondahl.

Tiffany Villeda, Iona Stewart, Samantha Quinones, Seen Cassell, Melissa Carlton, Ugo, Amanda Barker, Tricha Fely, Corrina Mayall, Ellen Swindall-Bailey, Alexis Abbott, Selena Kitt, Essie Munro, Anna Garcia-Centner, Biggi Ziegler, Jill Morrison, Alexia Falco, Kerrin Brittain, Ruth Roberts, Carol Ingham, Cynthia Powers, Tanya, Yolanda Pedroza, Belinda Jarrell, Miriam Loellgen, Pam Van Veen, Tammy Francis, Valerie Marshman.

1
______

Fiona Blache flicked on the pathetic yellow lights of her studio apartment which lit the space up enough to let her see but not enough to remove the dim, dark ambiance. She shuffled inside, kicking the door shut behind her before toeing off her shoes. *God, that's so much better.* Her feet killed her after that double shift and Mateen had been harping down her neck all day.

But it was a good day, she reminded herself. It was a very good day indeed because she'd been able to give a dragon shifter prince and his new fiancée some of the chocolate cupcakes she made. The pair had loved them a lot more than the cinnamon cakes Mateen had tried to get them to buy. Instead of peanut butter, she used chocolate cashew butter in the icing, just one of the many secret ingredients that she loved not telling Mateen.

The prince, a tall dragon shifter, Inferno Blackclaw the Fourth, enjoyed her chocolates so much that he bought an entire box. While she packed them up for him, he'd licked his fingers and stared at her, boring into her as though she were something special. That look was hot enough to...

Okay, down girl. He was an engaged prince, and she was just a peasant in his world. When they made their surprise visit to the bakery, Fiona had been covered in flour, wearing no makeup, with hair bunched up in a hair net and shoved under a white baker's cap. Someone like that didn't have a chance of being noticed next to the prince's fiancée, someone so out-and-out gorgeous that she could have been on a magazine cover. The woman was the perfect combination of curves, with a nice set of boobs and an ass that Fiona couldn't compete with even on her best-dressed days.

Fiona was naturally skinny, which was a good thing since she did have to taste test her own high calorie, high carb baked goods, but it also meant she had no ass to speak of, and her boobs could fit into a Martini glass with some room to spare.

Fiona smiled tiredly. *Whatever.* The prince just liked her cupcakes while she had been star-struck and smitten with his good looks. There hadn't been anything there but what was in her overactive imagination.

She set her purse down on the floor and let her hair out of the tight ponytail, reflecting on the dream that one day she'd own her own bakery. She wouldn't have to go through the motions like she did with Mateen and all the corners he cut. She was going to be able to proudly say that she had served the future King of Dragon shifters, and if that, plus her recipes, didn't bring in a lot of business, she didn't know what would.

Starving, she pulled out a cup of chicken ramen noodles and set it on the five inches of countertop space that was clear of papers, bills, magazines, spices, and recipe books stacked high on top of each other. They were only there because the shelf she got from IKEA was overflowing.

She put a kettle of hot water on and stuck some frozen veggies into her microwave.

Food would be ready in five minutes.

God, she was beat.

Dinner in hand, in a proper bowl, Fiona pulled her tiny coffee table close to her futon that doubled as her bed and leaned over her meal as she ate it.

She checked her bank balance on her phone as if she could somehow make the numbers go up from when she'd looked earlier today. She wasn't even close to having enough to open her bakery. Not when she factored in buying the ovens she would need, the ingredients, various cooking supplies, and the likelihood that it would take a full year before she was able to turn a profit.

Everyone said it took one to three years before a profit was had, which meant she needed even more money saved to be able to survive. Even if she could get a loan, she still wouldn't have enough.

But what if it didn't take a full year? The eldest prince of dragon shifters had walked into Mateen's bakery unannounced, on a whim, to see about possible cakes for his wedding, and there were always paparazzi following him. She remembered the cameras pointing through the glass as he ate her cupcakes, recording him licking his fingers...

Fiona shivered.

He was licking his fingers because the chocolate was good. Not because he was trying to send a message, no matter how much her body begged her to let him take her right there.

Focus. There had to be some way she could use the situation. Fiona closed down her bank's app and opened her social media accounts where she had a bit of a following that came over from her cooking blog and video channel.

She'd usually share her made-up recipes that weren't her super-secret specials, and she also gave sneak-peeks of the cookbook she was working on. Sometimes she got in a few advertising dollars from her blog or videos. Her following was small, but a viral video could be her ticket to something bigger.

There has to be some video of me online, something showing me serving the goddamn dragon prince.

She had to make sure people knew it was her, that Fiona Blache had made a dragon prince—a super-hot dragon prince with scorching dark eyes and a fantastic mouth—lick his fingers clean...while staring at her as if he wanted to lick her clean.

She shook her head. Now was not the time for that.

A quick trip to YouTube showed the videos were already up because, of course, they were. Fiona grinned. She'd never been so happy to know how ravenous the media could be, bloodsuckers that they were. She was going to have to find out how to rip a video off YouTube, edit it down, combine it with a reaction or commentary to ensure fair use, give it a good clickbait title, and upload it to her channel with her one hundred and thirteen subscribers. Then she could share it on the various other social networks and try to make it gain traction.

She tapped on the first one in the search results. She watched the recording of herself in front of the dragon prince and felt her heart jump with excitement. The prince's bride-to-be was on his other side; the camera barely picked up a hint of her. This video made it look as if it was just Fiona and Prince Inferno Blackclaw standing there, and her memory hadn't been playing tricks. Was he *ever* giving her a scorching eye.

Fiona released a tiny squeal, pressing the screen to her

chest because she couldn't bear to look much longer. Her face was hot, and not because she'd been leaning over the steam of her ramen cup a couple of seconds ago.

Damn. He was so good-looking, and he liked her food, and now she was going to make sure the entire world would see it!

She pulled the phone away from her chest, still smiling, but quirking her head to the side a little. She hadn't known Mateen gave an interview after the prince tasted her food. The smile slowly melted from her face when she realized what he was saying.

"Of course he would enjoy our cakes. My recipes are done and redone to perfection."

"Uh, no, that was *my* recipe."

The reporter spoke up. Fiona increased the volume so she could hear better.

"If Prince Inferno and his future princess want you to recreate those exact cakes for his wedding, would you be able to?"

"Of course. I hand make everything here by myself."

Fiona was standing now. "No. *I* hand make everything, and you sit on your ass and let the machines do all the work."

"Everything is done with love and care. If the prince wants more like this, if anyone wants more like this, they would do well to come down to my bakery, and they will see what I have to offer."

Fiona stared at her phone. She clutched it in two hands and screamed at the screen. She was raging and furious. The heat boiling inside her wouldn't be contained. He was taking credit for her recipe. He was going to have people coming to his bakery wanting what Fiona had made for the prince. His sales would probably shoot through the roof, leaving Fiona in the dust once more.

She screamed again. She kicked over the coffee table. Her big toe flared with pain, and she watched her ramen cup fly up high before coming back down almost in slow motion, but still too fast for her to do anything about it. She'd forgotten she had her food on the table. Her toe throbbed, the carpet was wet with her wasted dinner, and Fiona immediately started to cry as she sank on the floor. Her apartment was a mess, and she'd wasted food, and now she was going to have to clean it up while crying.

Okay, okay, no, this was...this was bullshit, but she wasn't going to let this stand. There was still something she could do. Her platform might be small, but she'd use her blog, even if it weren't read by many people, and her channel, which not too many people were subscribed to, and share the truth. If she posted that the recipe and the cupcakes were entirely hers, then at least it would stay on the internet forever. Some people would believe her, and ultimately, the prince was still eating in front of her, looking at her like that. The reporters didn't know what the prince was saying to her. She could say that he'd told her the cupcakes were amazing or something. It wouldn't entirely be a lie. He obviously liked what he was eating.

She quickly wrote off a post and published it, telling the world that those were her cupcakes, not Mateen's, and that she had made them that morning for regular customers when the prince and his fiancée dropped in. She didn't have pictures but promised to update the blog the minute she did, although she did post the recipe as proof.

Only when she finished could she breathe, but she still needed a video. It was dark outside. She needed natural light to do this well since she didn't have any lighting equipment. Would it be a better idea to make a low-quality video this one time? It was kind of an emergency.

Shit. She needed to clean up her soup first.

A knock sounded at the door. Fiona groaned. "Who is it?" She wasn't in the mood to hear about some cable package she didn't need.

No one answered as she scrambled to scoop her noodles and veggies back into their cup. She was going to have to use a whole roll of paper towels to soak up the broth.

The door banged this time. Fiona jumped and was so pissed off from everything that had just hit her that she yelled. "What? I don't want to buy anything. *Go away.*" She stood up, still angry, still thinking about how much she could get done before she had to get some sleep to go to work tomorrow.

If she could go back to work for Mateen, that fucker.

The door burst open just as Fiona was about to put the remains of her dinner into the sink. She dropped the cup in the sink just as several big men rushed into her tiny apartment.

Fiona screamed when the black, suffocating bag was shoved over her head.

2

———

"You realize this is creepy as fuck, right?"

Inferno hissed at his brother. "Shut up."

Blaze didn't shut up, and he didn't get down. He stood tall behind Inferno where anyone with a resistance to the cloaking spells Inferno had set up could look up and see them. "I mean, this is fucked up. You're creeping outside that girl's window, and you're engaged."

They weren't directly outside her window. They were on the roof of the opposite building looking at the window where she happened to live. When the light turned on, Inferno's heartrate spiked, and even though her curtains were closed, he couldn't take his eyes off the silhouette of the goddess as she did whatever her kind did at the end of a long day's work.

"It's not like Tinder and I actually love each other, and this is different. Did you *see* her hair?"

"Barely, it was all done up under that cap, and the reporters were too busy trying to stick their cameras in front of each other that I barely saw anything on my screen."

Blaze hadn't been there, so he couldn't know what

Inferno had felt. Something about the woman made him feel like he took a punch to the gut when he thought about the smile on her face as she told them about the cakes. Or about those sparkling green eyes, unlike any other green he'd ever seen—the color of the ocean under a bright sun—that followed him closely as he ate the food she offered. Green eyes were the rarest color, and hers were an even more unnatural shade.

And that *hair.*

He'd seen enough strands poking out from under that little white cap to know the color of it. It wasn't as if the paper hat had covered her entire head. It was bright red; a fire engine red, with streaks of flame orange, a reflection of fire as clear as anything he'd ever seen.

That woman was a rare creature. There was only one family that was supposed to have hair and eyes like that.

"She's an Istavan."

He heard Blaze's pacing footsteps stop behind him. Inferno wasn't looking at his brother, but he could imagine the other man staring at him, burning a hole in the back of his head.

"No fucking way."

"She is."

"That's impossible. That family died out years ago."

Inferno shook his head. "No, they just vanished. She's an Istavan. I can feel it."

"Wait." Blaze came up and knelt next to him. From the corner of Inferno's eye, he saw his brother watching him, but Inferno couldn't look away from that window. "Are you serious? You're really feeling this? I mean, you're feeling *it*?"

Inferno nodded.

"Oh my God, you should see your face right now. You're scaring me."

"What's wrong with my face?"

"That stupid smile you've got on it. And the fact that you haven't once looked at me this whole conversation. Are you sure about this?"

Inferno nodded. "Positive. She's my mate."

There were only a handful of human families that could produce offspring with dragons, and every few years, the families were cycled through. This was supposed to be the time for the Istavans to produce a child that would be mated with Inferno. It was just the way it worked. Inferno's mother had been from the Montgomery family, so it was the Istavan family's turn.

The problem was that the family had been missing for the last five hundred years. Every time it came around for the Istavans to step forward, the noble dragon families had to marry another dragon or they would simply waste away alone. Either way, they went without their natural mate.

Inferno had known from the beginning that as the oldest son he was supposed to be mated to an Istavan, but that there was no one in their line for him. Everyone in his family had known this, which was why he'd grown up knowing he would marry his distant cousin, Tinder, instead.

Inferno had thought he was strong. He'd felt he could handle this hand he had been dealt because he sure as hell wasn't about to let himself waste away longing for a mate he'd never met. But there, in a tiny bakery that he walked into on a whim, in a city he was only visiting to make good with the humans, his mate was waiting to serve him cupcakes.

What were the odds of that?

"Okay, so if you're sure about this, what are you going to do? What about Tinder? What about Aunt Charrling?"

"What about them?"

"Charrling might take it easier, she'll know about the importance of the family lines, but you know Tinder—"

A distant scream cut off his brother before he could finish. Inferno's spine stiffened. He spread his wings out and jumped off the roof.

"Hey, fucker! Wait for me!"

Inferno ignored his brother and flew across to the other building. He hit the wall next to the Istavan's window. His claws dug into the cement and brick, punching holes and letting him stick in place. He looked through the window, cursing the curtain that was in the way, but it was thin, and he could see a touch more than shadow this time. He got a hint of color through the white material, and with how close he was, he could hear...

Crying.

Inferno's heart clenched. His heart never clenched. Tinder cried for things in front of him many times in her attempt to manipulate him into buying gifts or spending more time with her, but his chest never constricted the way it did now.

"What's happening? Is she crying?"

Inferno glanced up at his brother, who stared at him upside down above the window.

"Clearly she is, just shut up for a minute."

Inferno listened carefully to the sobs that came from inside the window. He couldn't understand what she would be crying over, but these were not the soft, delicate sobs that Tinder made when she was looking for attention.

The crying stopped a moment later, replaced with sniffles. Inferno tried looking through the window again. He thought he could make out the figure inside cleaning something up off the floor. That changed when a hard bang came from her door.

"Who is it?" He heard her ask.

The banging happened again, and his mate made a growling noise that made Inferno proud. "What? I don't want to buy anything. *Go away.*"

She knew how to handle people annoying her at her door. He loved this more and more. When he took her out of here to woo her, it would be an interesting match.

A crash sounded, and his mate screamed.

Inferno's lungs briefly seized with the panic of hearing such a noise. He and his brother exchanged a look in a single split-second before crashing through the window. Inferno was momentarily blinded by the yellow light of the room that hit him worse than the street lamps outside. Luckily, his vision cleared quickly, and he hissed at the sight of four men in black suits and masks around his mate. They'd placed a black bag over her head, and one man was holding a knife to her throat.

The room itself froze. The men stared at Inferno through the holes in their black masks while Inferno's mind raced to find a solution to the problem of the knife.

"If you even think of putting that blade any closer to her throat, I swear you won't be able to run fast enough. If you put it down and walk out of here, I'll let the lot of you live."

Not that there was any chance that he'd let them live after this. No fucking way was that going to happen.

The idiot with the knife pulled it away a few inches; more than enough space for Inferno to act.

His hand went for the blade he kept holstered to his side. Inferno was usually quick, but as he threw the knife, his heart was seized with the worst sort of fear. If he'd been too late, too slow, the man's edge would connect to her throat, and it would all be over.

Inferno's throwing blade landed in the man's eye, mercifully far enough away from his mate for his heart to start beating again. The man yanked backward, screaming a wretched noise, prompting the other men around him to pull their weapons. Blaze responded by releasing a roar that made the walls around them vibrate, but Inferno made no sound at all. The rage within him blistered dangerously quiet as he withdrew another throwing knife.

The men broke formation, but they didn't charge the dragon brothers. Instead, they bolted toward the door. Inferno blinked as he looked to Blaze.

"Did those idiots just run away?"

"Looks like it. See if you can catch them. I need—"

"I know, I'm on it." Blaze was swift, neatly jumping over the woman as he ran for the door after the men.

Inferno fell to his knees in front of her. Her shirt was torn open, revealing a white cotton bra that was slightly crooked on her breasts, as if she'd given quite the struggle against her attackers.

His primary concern was the bag on her head though and making sure she was still breathing. They'd tied the bag tightly around her neck, pressing the string into the sooth, fragile skin of her throat.

Inferno pulled his claws out and neatly cut the string, stretching the bag open and drawing it off her head. The rope left behind a deep red mark, but he didn't see blood anywhere. Not from the line or the knife that Captain Fuck-face had been holding against her.

The green eyes that stared up into his were wide and frightened. Inferno was a prince, the first in line to inherit the North American Kingdom of dragons, and as such, he had extensive training in self-defense, first aid, leading armies into battle, and reassuring his people. Yet in this moment, he had no idea what to do.

She was motionless but alive. Everything had happened too quickly, but he could still see life in her eyes. She wasn't gone from this world. Not yet.

Inferno finally remembered his training. It only took the one breath and slight compression to remind her lungs what they were supposed to be doing.

She convulsed and coughed beneath him. He pulled back as his mate turned to her side, clutching her throat, coughing and gasping for breath. He saw tears spill from her eyes as she sucked back another breath, and another, each seeming to come easier than the last.

Inferno's chest felt like it was held in a vice. He had to touch her. Had to hold her after coming so close to losing her. It was too much to nearly lose her after he'd only just managed to find her.

He placed his hands on her shoulders, pulled her into his lap, and wrapped his arms around her. His emotions bubbled over, coming out as a laugh, one that sounded a little maniacal, even to him. Against his body, hers felt so small and fragile, like a rag doll.

Her breath wheezed. Inferno didn't realize right away that she was speaking to him. "Thank you."

He kissed her beautiful red hair, damp and cold with sweat as it was from being in that hideous black bag. As much as she was trying to catch her breath and bearings, he too was trying to compose himself. He was unable to stop the feeling that he had almost lost something as essential to him as a limb. Even more so. She was something he couldn't live without. "You're coming with me now, sweetheart."

Because there was no way in hell he was going to risk something like this happening again.

3

Fiona remembered a black bag being shoved on her head, but then nothing else after those horrifying seconds when she couldn't breathe.

The next thing she knew she shot up and gasped, her hand coming to her throat, desperate to yank the bag off.

But there was no bag. There was nothing on her face. She was...she was breathing. She was all right. Her heart slammed against her ribs as if it was trying to break out of there forcefully, but she was all right and breathing. She placed a hand over her heart, as though she could calm it down with the pressure.

She immediately noticed the difference in fabric her hand was touching.

She looked down at herself. Her clothes didn't just feel different. They were different. This was some soft, fancy stuff she was wearing. *Is this...cashmere? Do they even make pajamas out of cashmere?*

She almost couldn't stop touching it; it was so soft and comfortable. It took her another couple of seconds before she realized, *holy shit*, this was definitely not her bedspread.

This wasn't her bed. She didn't even have a bed, just the futon. This mattress with its fluffy quilts felt like she was lying on pillows that had been placed on top of even puffier pillows.

Fiona was afraid to look up and around, but she did it anyway. The dark room had a few strategically placed lamps on the wall. Their glow was small and soft, like the night-light she used to avoid stepping on things when she had to use the bathroom in the middle of the night. Only there were more than one of these lights, and they weren't plugged into wall sockets.

The room was bigger than her whole apartment. It had to be at least three times the size. The ceiling was higher, too. High enough that another apartment could have been put up there, and Fiona had only been able to tell that because she had to lean outside the canopy bed to have a look.

She took quick stock of herself, her hands sliding around her body, searching. Okay, she needed to calm down. She wasn't tied down, and she didn't feel injured in any way, but that didn't mean she wasn't a prisoner. She didn't know what these people wanted from her, but what-ever it was she was *not* about to let any weird shit happen to her.

Shit. Had someone seen her on TV making eyes at the dragon prince?

Was this their way of teaching her a lesson?

She had to get out of here. She needed to get out of this bed, find her clothes, and go.

Fiona hooked her legs over the side of the bed. She nearly groaned when her feet touched the soft carpet. God, this place was strange, and she didn't like how she'd come to be here, but damn, this bed was warm and comfortable. How stupid was it that she didn't want to leave it?

Yeah, pretty stupid. She needed to get a move on.

There were slippers next to the bed, fuzzy and a matching shade of pink to her luxurious pajamas. *Not exactly what you'd find in a mature woman's closet...*

Which didn't stop Fiona from wanting to wear them. If they were anything like the carpet and pajamas she wore, they probably felt like stepping on cotton balls.

No! What the hell was her problem? *Okay, focus.* She'd been attacked and kidnapped. If her attackers came back in here and saw her awake, what was she going to do if they wanted to choke her out again?

Clothes. Where were her clothes?

There was an honest to God wardrobe to her right. She opened it up, shocked to find it empty, even the little drawers beneath it. There was another set of drawers, something that looked as if it was made out of solid wood, nothing at all like the set Fiona had been eyeballing from IKEA. It was also empty.

Why would someone have a big room like this with so much expensive furniture and not bother filling it with anything?

Fiona tensed, a rush of irritation and annoyance flooding over her the likes of which she couldn't entirely explain.

"Is this a *guest* room?"

The idea seemed ludicrous and insulting. Again, she couldn't fully explain it even to herself. Fiona lived in a bachelor apartment. She would have loved to have enough money to have a single bedroom. It was her dream to one day have enough money to buy a small house with an office for her and a spare bedroom for friends and family visitors though she wouldn't keep it filled with furniture that would never be used. She'd still find something to do with her guest room instead of just leaving it empty, collecting dust while waiting for someone to use it.

Maybe I'm just jealous.

Fiona went to the window, pulling aside the heavy curtains, wondering if they cost about as much as her month's rent.

She saw soft orange, pink, and blue glows in the distance that meant the sun was about to come up. As a baker, Fiona had a high internal alarm clock. *If the sun's coming up, I should have been at Mateen's an hour ago. He's probably having a fit right now.*

But she couldn't bring herself to feel panic over that.

Maybe it was because of how he took credit for her cupcakes, or maybe it was the kidnapping putting everything into perspective, but she knew there was no way she'd ever go back to working for him. Not now.

That stupid asshole.

Letting her eyes take in the beautifully manicured and vast gardens, Fiona saw that her kidnapper was clearly loaded. She'd heard about humans being kidnapped and sold to wealthy dragons, and that it could be a lucrative business. If that was what was happening, was she at the home of the rich kidnapper, or already at the home of the human-buying dragon scum?

Fiona quickly closed the window when a man in a black suit and shades, his hands behind his back, looked up at her. There was no way he hadn't seen that. They'd looked right at each other, and even if by some miracle he hadn't seen her, he would definitely see the rustle of the curtains. "Shit."

Okay, time to forget about her clothes, but she was going to need some shoes.

Fiona eyed the pink slippers.

She rushed to them and slipped them on. Her eyes rolled to the back of her head. God, these were stupidly comfortable.

Whatever. It was time to go. Fiona sprinted to the wide door that, just like the furniture, could have been carved from a solid piece of wood. She didn't want to think about how much money the door handles cost.

Maybe she should take something. Theft wasn't her thing, but if she could take something from the people who'd kidnapped her, then it would only be fair play.

And it wouldn't hurt to find a weapon while she was at it.

Right, back to the drawing board.

Fiona rushed to the nightstand, yanking it open, and holy God, was she lucky or what? Like every other piece of furniture she'd so far checked, it was mostly empty, but there was a pad of paper and a pen. She opened the cap and saw it was the sort of thing designed to look like a dip pen, but wasn't.

Sharp. She could use this to defend herself, and maybe sell it for a little cash.

Might as well get paid for her trouble.

Okay, her heart raced, but she could handle this. Fiona went back to the door. She sucked in a deep breath before turning the handle as slowly and carefully as possible.

As if there was a baby in the room she didn't want to wake.

Careful, careful.

The knob clicked a little when she managed to get it open. Fiona cringed. Fuck. Why was nothing ever silent when she needed to be quiet? Was it one of the rules of the world?

No alarms sounded. No one burst through the door and slammed her back down onto the ground, and no black bags came.

Fiona swallowed. She pulled herself out of that memory before she let it fling her into a full-on panic attack.

Stay alert and stay aware. That was her mission.

Of course, the door also creaked when she pulled it open. A long, loud noise that seemed to get louder the slower she went.

Fiona flipped the pen in her hand so she held it like a knife. She sucked up her courage and took a small, easy step out into the empty hall. She glanced down one way, then jumped when she peered down the other and spotted a man less than two feet away from her. She fell against the other side of the door. The man didn't move. He had a single brow raised as he looked at her, almost with concern in his eyes.

"Are you all right, Miss?"

Fiona said nothing. She held her pen as she stared at him. He wore a black suit with sunglasses and an earpiece as if he was in the secret service or something.

If she went for his face, he would have to defend his eyes. That might help her get away. Would the slippers stay on her feet if she ran as hard and fast as she could outside?

The man smiled at her. She saw now that he was young, with a boyish face and straight white teeth showing out from his quirked lips. "You're safe here, and you don't need to worry. The people who hurt you are gone."

Fiona blinked. "W-What?"

That cute smile faded slightly. "You were attacked, weren't you? Your throat is bleeding."

"It is?"

Fiona brought her hand up to her neck. When she pulled it back, there was just a tiny bit of blood there, not enough to worry over. "I must have scratched myself when I—hey!"

The young man sprung fast, so swiftly Fiona didn't have a chance to lash out at him, to make him back off before he had his hands around her wrist, pulling her hand up high before he forced her fingers open and took her pen.

He danced back effortlessly when she swung her fist at his face, knocking her knuckles against the doorframe. The burst of pain in her hand shot up her arm. "Oh, God." Fiona held her hand between her legs, crouching down to shelter her hand from more abuse, even though she'd been the reason why it had happened in the first place.

"I am very sorry, miss," said the guy who was no longer looking quite so cute. "But I can't have you walking around threatening members of staff. Does your hand hurt? I can take you to the physician."

He reached down and grabbed her by the elbow. Fiona yanked her arm away. "Don't touch me." She pulled herself to her feet to stop him from making any more moves to help her.

He raised his hands and backed off. "If that's what you want, miss, but at the very least I need to tell His Highness that you're awake."

That caught her attention. Fiona stopped squeezing her hand so tight and looked hard at the guy in front of her. "What did...his highness? As in Prince Inferno? You're saying Prince Inferno kidnapped me?"

The young guard cocked his head to the side a little. "No, not really. While he did relocate you without your consent, it was after you'd been attacked, and he didn't trust the human authorities to handle you properly."

The enormous room she'd just been in and the vast lawn she'd seen outside in the coming dawn suddenly made a little more sense.

"Are you saying I'm in the royal palace?"

The guard smiled so wide Fiona almost looked away from how bright it was. "Indeed you are, miss. Welcome."

"Does the prince have a palace in Ottawa that I don't know about?"

The guard shook his head. "No, miss. You are in Inferno City."

Inferno City, which happened to be a whole time zone away from her home.

A sound escaped her as she sank to the floor again, trying to wrap her mind around this new situation.

4

___

Inferno marched down the vast halls of his home. This place was too fucking big. It had been a maze as a child. He could almost get lost in it. As an adult, it was just a pain in the ass to get around.

The message he got from the guards outside his mate's window claiming she was awake had been enough to make him end the conversation he'd been having with his aunt and Tinder. The looks on their faces when he'd broken off the engagement were something he would very much like to forget, but that didn't seem likely to happen.

Both had been sullen. Tinder hadn't cried, which was odd because Inferno had expected it. She hadn't appeared angry either. Perhaps it was just the shock. She would come out of it in time and lash out. She usually did whenever there was something that disappointed her.

Inferno knew it was a dick move to leave Ember alone to deal with their relatives. Ember was usually a generous brother, but Inferno knew there was a very real chance he'd get his ass kicked for abandoning him like that. It was Inferno's drama, after all.

His phone buzzed again. He glanced down at the SOS message. His grip tightened on the phone as he hurried even quicker to the guest wing. His temper flared with his impatience. *I should have kept her close to me, not across the castle.*

It seemed to take forever to get there, and he heard a shriek just before he turned the final corner and saw the woman and some of his security staff down the hall. "What is going on?" His roar carried down to the figures, who all stilled at the sound of it.

"Your Highness!"

Fiona, whose name he'd had a chance to learn while she slept, was sitting on the ground, rocking herself. Eric, the one he'd assigned as her primary guard, was crouched next to her, but it was the second guard, with his hand on his Taser, who Inferno was primarily concerned with.

"I don't think you're going to need that weapon against a frightened guest."

The man tensed. "She took a swing at Eric, and then had another outburst, sir. I was just standing prepared."

"You really couldn't handle her? She can't weigh more than a hundred pounds soaking wet; you're telling me you're scared of her?"

"Hey!"

Inferno looked back at her. "There's no shame in being as vicious as a kitten."

"Double hey!"

He liked her. He liked that she had some spunk, but then he frowned, that red haze clouding over his vision once more. "Is that blood on you? Who made her bleed?" He hissed at the guards, and once again they cowered.

Inferno looked to Eric, who was only just now helping his mate back onto her feet. "You?"

His eyes flew wide. "What? No, your highness, I wouldn't do that." He stepped away from her as if his mate was suddenly made of acid. "I wouldn't do that."

Fiona lifted one hand to her neck and looked at the knuckles on her other. "I must have scratched at my neck while I was sleeping. Nightmares about what happened last night, most likely, and then this," she indicated her bloody knuckles "was the result of me trying to take on Eric, and landing a blow onto your great doorframe instead."

"You did this?"

There wasn't a lot of blood that he could see, but he wanted a closer inspection. He walked up to her. Fiona's eyes widened. She backed up, but the wall was immediately behind her. Inferno reached out and snatched her hand, pulling it up to have a look at her knuckles. They were more scraped than injured in a way that would require bandaging, and he couldn't discern any splinters. He turned his attention to her throat, having a look for himself.

"Turn your head to the side."

She blinked those big green eyes up at him and didn't move.

Inferno sighed. He gently pushed her red and orange flame hair away from her shoulder. The red mark left from the bag's string had swollen up and bruised, but he could also now see nail marks where she must have been scratching at it in her sleep. He didn't like any of it, not the reminder of what she'd been through, and not the idea that she was still fighting off those attackers in her nightmares. He couldn't do anything about that, though, so he'd focus on what he could fix, starting with getting her wounds tended.

He took her by the arm. "Come with me. We have some things to take care of."

Fiona didn't move. "Why did you kidnap me?"

Inferno paused. He blinked down at her rather stupidly. "Did you hear me? We have somewhere to be."

"No. Not until you tell me why I'm here."

He jerked back. Did she...? She had. She'd made a *command*.

Inferno glared back at Eric and the other guard, remembering they were there. They seemed to be collectively attempting to pretend this whole thing wasn't happening since they weren't allowed to leave without Inferno's say-so.

"I will explain myself, but only because this is a new situation for you, and it is understandable that you would be upset by your attack, and then waking in an unfamiliar location. I took you for your protection." Fuck. Why did it have to sound so lame even to his ears?

She stared at him as if waiting for more. "That's...that's it?"

Inferno frowned. "What do you mean, *that's it?*"

"You said you were going to explain."

"I did."

"That's not much of an explanation. Eric said something about you not trusting human authorities. Does that mean you know who attacked me? And why?"

Was this a thing with human women?

"You were attacked by men who tried to kill you. I would not stand for that." Inferno waved his hand out to the guards and the wealth around them. "This will provide you with more protection than you could receive in your apartment building, or at your little bakery."

She looked away, frowning slightly. She seemed to be thinking about his answer, but Inferno was uncertain what she needed to consider.

"But why not just call the police? Why did you have to take me out of my home? Out of my city? Not that I'm not grateful; I am, believe me." Something dark and panicky danced in her eyes as if she was reliving her attack. "But isn't it kind of extreme to have me here?"

"This is your home now."

Now she blinked up at him. "What? What are you talking about?"

He couldn't stand this for much longer. "You will come with me now, then I will answer more of your questions," he added as an afterthought. Gentle. He had to be gentle. She was a human, and she was supposed to be frightened and finicky after her ordeal.

"Uh, sire?"

Inferno looked towards Eric. He held out a pair of Flare's slippers. Inferno had asked his little sister to borrow them for his mate, since she had a tremendous collection and certainly had some she wouldn't mind parting with.

"I suppose you kicked these off while attacking the guards?"

Fiona's face flamed up. The red in her cheeks was a different shade than that in her hair, but Inferno thought that Fiona looked positively lovely. Her flame hair was a tousled mess around her shoulders, and he loved the look of her cheeks and nose bursting with color.

He handed her the slippers. She took them with a mumbled thanks.

He couldn't resist. Inferno took his mate by the chin and lifted her face. He pressed his mouth to hers, feeling the sudden tension in her body, followed by her hands touching his chest.

Fiona shoved Inferno, breaking the chaste kiss.

"So this is really what it's about? So much for wanting to protect me. You're probably the one who sent those men to kidnap me so I'd become one more woman for your harem, isn't that right, oh mighty dragon lord?"

He just kissed her. Was that real? Or had she only imagined it?

And had she just shoved him away and berated him?

They'd stood locked in an awful stare down for just a moment before he took her arm and guided her away from her room. She was too afraid to object. He'd kidnapped her, and he was a very powerful man. The two guards would be able to take her out in an instant if he didn't want to get his hands dirty. She needed to toe the line better if she wanted any answers and wanted any chance of getting out of there.

This had to be a dream. Fiona was walking in a daze. That stuff she'd thought happened when those people broke into her apartment had to be fake. That stuff didn't happen in real life, and it seemed like such a haze.

She'd been drooling all over Inferno just the day before, and she was supposed to believe this was somehow her new reality? The most gorgeous royal in the world had rescued her, whisked her off to his palace, and then kissed her. Without her consent. And while he was engaged. "I'm starting to think I might be dead."

"No, not quite, thank God."

She looked up at him. "Then...why did those people try to...they came into my apartment, and they tried to..."

Fiona hadn't been able to see when they'd thrown that suffocating back over her head. She hadn't been able to breathe much when they'd tightened the cord on her either, but she could remember exactly what it felt like when they'd grabbed her.

Inferno stopped suddenly, his hands on her shoulders as

he stepped in front of her. The fact that this big man was suddenly in her personal space threw her off for a hair of a second, but she wasn't in her apartment, and there weren't a bunch of men on top of her trying to kill her.

"I will never let that happen to you. Not ever again. I will find the ones responsible for what happened to you, and I will pour every resource into seeing they are brought to justice."

Red scales suddenly appeared on Inferno's face and neck, as if just under the last layer of skin at first, then they were the top layer. His eyes blazed, his grip on her shoulders tightening.

His reaction calmed her. It should have made her tense up again, but it didn't. It made her feel *better*. "Why would you do this, for me of all people?" She had to know. The need was too strong. "You say you want to protect me, but why? Are my cupcakes that good? If you want more, I'm happy to make them, but I don't want to be your side piece."

"Side piece?"

Her voice went unexpectedly small, and she almost couldn't say that last part at all. "Is it just because you're rich? Because you want to mess with me? I can't think of any real reason as to why you would fly me out here unless you're bored and used to getting what you want."

"I am used to getting what I want."

Fiona exhaled a hard half laugh. "Well, at least you're honest."

"I am." Inferno leaned in, allowing Fiona to see the fire in his eyes. A literal fire. It burned and crackled, sucking her in and warming her from the inside out. "So believe me when I tell you that you'll never be a side piece. My engagement to Tinder is off, now that I've found my destined mate, you, and I'm prepared to give you my name and my power if you would do me the honor of taking it."

She blinked stupidly up at him. The fantasy part of her brain wanted to jump at him, accept what he said at face value, and ride off into the sunset with her happily ever after.

That wasn't what she blurted out. "What if I don't want to take it?"

He looked at her long and hard. "Then I will wait for you to accept, but we will both remain here."

"Here." She looked around.

"Where else would you stay when you need protection from a threat?"

Fiona couldn't believe it. A dragon prince was kidnaping her.

5

His mate didn't appear happy with the knowledge that she would be staying in his vast home. Inferno reasoned that it was nothing more than a case of shock. She couldn't believe her new surroundings, or that this was all now hers. Considering the tiny apartment Inferno had pulled her out of, he couldn't blame her for that.

He was no fool. He knew there was more to it than just the grandeur of his dwelling. He may be a dragon prince, but he still understood well enough that her surroundings were, in fact, not what was making her speechless.

"The men you met will be keeping you safe while we look into who attacked you. Eric will be in charge. He's young but loyal and talented. He'll see to your safety."

"Eric? The guy who was outside my room? Blond hair, sunglasses, and the earpiece?"

Inferno couldn't help but smile at the ridiculous description. "That would be him?"

"Is he human?"

Inferno glanced down at Fiona. "No. He has dragon blood."

"He does?"

"This shocks you?" He couldn't understand why.

Fiona glanced away quickly, color rising in her cheeks. God, with her red and orange hair, she was the loveliest thing he'd ever seen in his life, and she was an Istavan. She was his mate.

"I just...I always thought that dragons had fiery sounding names, you know? Your name is Inferno, for God's sakes."

Inferno chuckled. "Yes, and while I do like my name, sometimes something a little more normal would have been better. Like William or Phillip. Those are perfectly royal sounding names. They just don't keep to certain old dragon traditions."

Fiona smiled softly at that. "I guess that makes sense." She paused. "So, about this whole, I'm your mate and I live here now thing... You know you can't keep me here, right?"

"I'm fairly positive that I can."

Fiona stopped walking beside him, forcing Inferno to stop and look back at her.

"What is it?" Her glare and clenched hands were concerning.

"What do you mean, *what is it*? It's kidnapping, that's what it is. Which, by the way, is totally illegal."

"And I am a prince."

"So you're above the law?"

He smiled at her.

She threw her hands in the air, then pushed her fingers through her hair. "Unbelievable. You can't just force me to stay here."

Inferno frowned at that. "Do you feel this is bothersome for you? Being here?"

"*Of course it is.* I need to go home. Back to my life. Back to my job."

"The job where you accused the owner of theft?"

Fiona jerked back. "What?"

Inferno pulled out his phone. "You posted this just before the attack, correct?"

He held out the phone, allowing her to see her handiwork.

Fiona glared at him. "So you started stalking all my profiles, is that it?"

Inferno lifted a brow. "You're my intended mate. Of course, I'd want to find out all I could about you. Strictly above board, that is. I wouldn't want to invade your privacy. And this tidbit of information was posted on your blog for all the public to see, which makes my reading it hardly stalking."

"Whatever. All right?" She swiped her hand out, trying to take the phone, but Inferno pulled back as Fiona danced around him, desperate to take it out of his hands. "It doesn't matter anyway. Mateen is an asshole, but he's my boss, and I need that job."

"Why work for him at all?"

"Because everywhere else I tried to get a job had me on the register too much or cleaning toilets. I'm a baker, and Mateen lets me bake. That's the point of working for him. Then you walked in and—"

Fiona's word cut off. Inferno saw her lovely green eyes glaze over. She'd gone somewhere else. It brought out all the protective instincts Inferno had within him. The idea that someone, anyone, had put their hands on her and the only reason Inferno had been there to stop it was through some sheer dumb luck made the dragon side of himself wild with rage.

He squashed it down. Inferno curled his arms around Fiona's shoulders, holding her snuggly but not too tight. After her ordeal, he didn't dare risk her falling back into that state of fear. He wouldn't let that happen.

"I am so sorry that happened to you."

She was small in his arms, which did nothing to help stop those protective instincts from rising inside him. She was fragile, and someone had tried to snuff out that life. Someone he was going to find and make suffer a long and painful death.

No, death would be too good. He could think of worse.

"It's over now." It wasn't over. He was lying. "They can't hurt you anymore. Not while you're here." He couldn't guarantee such a thing until he had the ones responsible for this in front of him, and he tore out their throats with his bare hands.

"Why did they do that?"

Inferno sighed. He suspected it had something to do with him. What else could it have been? He couldn't say such a thing to her. Not when she was adamant that she shouldn't be here at all.

"Whoever they were, they will pay, kitten. Believe me. I won't rest until they have been brought to justice. Until then, try not to concern yourself with the bakery." He couldn't help a wry smile. "From what I saw of that post, you didn't much enjoy working for him anyway."

Fiona groaned. She buried her face against Inferno's chest, which he had to admit, he enjoyed. "I can't believe I did that. He's going to fire me for sure. I should have been in this morning."

"I told you not to worry about it. I will cover whatever costs you have."

Fiona tensed. She pulled back just enough to look up into his eyes. He could see the want within them, the desire to take the protection he offered, but she shook her head, the reluctance obvious. "N-No, I can't ask you to do that. I mean, I am so very grateful that you saved me and everything, but..." She must have just noticed that she was in his arms. She pulled back, the flush to her cheeks as bright as ever. "I can't just have you pay for me. That's not right either."

Inferno cocked his head to the side a little, eyeing his mate from bottom to top. He brought his hand up to rub at his jaw. "Very interesting."

"What is?"

"You," he said. "You must be the first person in the history of my life not to accept money when it's offered to you. No one has turned down rewards or promises of cash before."

Fiona briefly bit her lips together. "Right, well, I'm trying not to be a greedy asshole here."

"So you will accept my gift if I offer it enough?"

The look on her face suggested she was already having trouble turning it down. Inferno knew, at that moment, that this woman wasn't used to generosity, but could learn how to accept it in time.

Right. But he had to remember that humans had their fair amount of pride. Judging by her small apartment, her job couldn't have paid all that well. People did not often choose such circumstances. She might have claimed that she chose that job over others because her boss let her work in the kitchen all she wanted, but he could tell she would have dropped that job like she was coming down for a hard landing if anything remotely better presented itself.

And an idea came to mind — a way to present the situation that might allow her to accept it better.

"This is not charity. This is an assignment."

"A job?"

He nodded. "Indeed. An arrangement. You will stay in my home and accept payment, enough for you to start your bakery by the end of the deal if you perform to my expectations."

Her green eyes flew wide. "How did you—*oh*," she said, deflating a little when he raised and wiggled his phone. "You've had a lot of time to read over my blog, haven't you?"

"And watch some of your more interesting videos."

She swallowed. Inferno watched, transfixed, as her throat worked. "What could you possibly want me to do for enough money to start my own business?"

"The answer is simple. You will enter into a marriage contract with me, and carry my heirs, becoming the mother of the future lords of the dragon kingdom."

6

———

Fiona couldn't understand why Inferno appeared so pleased with himself

"This shocks you. Good," he said. "It would shock most to be given so much, but as my mate, you more than deserve it."

Fiona shook her head. "I'm not mating with you."

The smile slipped from his face. He tilted his head to the side. "Is there something you object to?"

"I object to the idea that you're just going to assume I'll be your mate and have your dragon babies. That's not the way it works in real life."

"It is how it works in real life. This was the way it was always done."

"Not for humans."

"You are no ordinary human."

That threw her off even more. "Even if I were, what of your fiancée?"

"I told you, my cousin, Tinder, was just a fill-in. Now that my true mate has been discovered, she's free of her obligation to marry me."

He smiled at that, then offered her his hand. Fiona hesitated, and against her better judgment, she took hold of it. It felt warm in a good way, and a tingling sensation rushed up her arm and into her spine, but that wasn't what made her shiver. It was the sudden pulse of pleasure that hit her down below, between her legs. Holy shit, just touching his hand almost felt as if he had his mouth on her nipples, and the shocks of pleasure were sudden.

She wanted to pull away, she almost did, but she couldn't.

"You'll get used to that," Inferno offered, looping her arm through his so she could hold onto him as she walked.

Fiona walked, though it was in a daze. "What did you do to me?"

She glanced up as Inferno frowned. "Don't make me out to be some sort of villain. I did nothing to you. This is instinct."

"What?"

He went back to smiling as if he was the most excited man in the world or a kid at Christmas. "Instinct. The more I touch you, or the longer I touch you, the more you will be affected. Do not worry; it's happening to me, too."

She hadn't even thought of that. Fiona knew she wasn't horrible to look at; in fact, she could look pretty good when she had the opportunity to do her hair and makeup, but she also didn't inspire men like this to shiver with lust and pleasure either.

She glanced up at him. Fiona felt like she could barely contain it. Was he feeling this same shivery lust for her that she felt for him? She suddenly, in that moment, remembered the way he'd licked her chocolate sauce in the bakery, and she had to bite back a groan. Yeah, maybe she could believe he was struggling with this, too. Why was that knowledge so intoxicating?

Inferno continued. "Introductions will have to be made. I'll avoid my aunt and cousin for the time being. I imagine they are not happy with me, and with what is happening between us, but my brothers will be excited to meet you."

Fiona hardly saw the halls around her anymore, the bright lights, and the expensive furnishings that had been placed along the walls to act more for decoration than to be used. She could only look up at him. "Why would your brothers be excited to meet me? What's going on? I need..." She shivered as another rush of pleasure hit her right in her sex, making it throb as if there was an actual hand down there, touching her, trying to make her sing. She clenched her teeth. "I need to know."

"And I will tell you." Inferno gazed down at her. "You're not my captive. You are free to roam wherever you wish."

"Just not back home?"

He looked away. Fiona got the feeling she'd hurt him, but his face remained a stoic mask.

"Considering the men who tried to kill you, is that something you want?"

Fiona bit her lips together. "Don't suppose you'd let me take some bodyguards with me or anything, would you?"

Inferno laughed, shaking his head. "Not at the moment, no."

Not at the moment. Okay, maybe there was something here for her to work with.

They passed by several end tables that were probably made of solid wood. On them were either expensive looking lamps, or vases that probably cost more than two months of Fiona's rent combined, and each had flowers of absolutely perfect shapes inside. She'd thought they were fake at first, but then remembered where they were. The palace where the prince of dragons lived with his family wouldn't have fake flowers, and the smell they emitted was something even the best artificial ones couldn't replicate.

Inferno brought her down another large hallway. This one had all the doors shut, and all the window curtains pulled closed, though some soft light did still manage to break through. The halls were mostly lit by the lamps on the walls and those end tables, along with what had to be crystal chandeliers above her head.

"This is crazy."

"I'm glad you approve."

She did, but that didn't mean she wanted to live here. Inferno was handsome as hell and sure, touching him in any skin-to-skin way for this long made her want to jump his bones, but that was entirely beside the point.

Inferno stepped up to two double doors. "I asked my brothers to meet me here. It's early, but they will have likely shown up by now."

Fiona tensed. "Already?"

She was about to meet the other dragons in the royal family, and she wasn't ready, dressed as she was.

"They will not hurt you. Blaze was there with me, helping me to rescue you."

That seemed to make the heat in her neck and face even worse. "I can't meet them looking like this; I'm wearing pajamas."

"And you look beautiful in them." He brought her hand to his mouth and kissed her knuckles. He didn't kiss her on the mouth this time, but she was sure she would never get used to that feeling she got whenever his mouth touched her. The intense heat was like a fire beneath her skin and between her legs. She wanted to have sex with this man.

The mating thing was something she didn't entirely understand, but she wanted the sex.

"I'm going to fly apart."

"Don't do that," Inferno said, chuckling. "Come. They will be happy to see you."

He opened only one of the double doors, then held it open for her so she could walk in first. No one had ever held a door open for her. Well, strangers had at times, but no one she'd dated. It seemed weird, and it probably wasn't helping with her plan to look independent and capable of handling herself, but she liked it, and she allowed him to do it.

There were people waiting inside. It looked like a conference room that was used to make business decisions, and two other men were sitting at the table in the middle, their feet up, chatting with each other while their phones and tablets were propped up around them.

They straightened up at the sight of Fiona and Inferno entering the room.

"I knew you would be early," Inferno said.

"Not like it's that early. Is that her?"

"This is indeed her."

Fiona knew who he was because of the pictures. That was Ember. He was the youngest of the brothers, but just as tall and wide in the shoulders. He was even bigger in real life than was on a TV screen or in a magazine.

Ember stepped forward. He wore a suit, tailored so that it fit him perfectly, but it was casual in the way that it wasn't buttoned up, and lacked a tie. He held out his hand. "Pleasure to make your acquaintance. My name is Ember Blackclaw."

She expected him to add on *the Fourth*, as well as his title as prince, but he didn't. His introduction was a lot more polite than what she was used to getting, but not the stuffy thing she would have expected to come from a prince either.

"It's good to meet you." She was definitely nervous. "Should I curtsey?"

Ember pulled back, his eyes wide, then he laughed. "No, please don't. I hate that people have to do that out in public. In here, please, by all means, never curtsey to me. Or to either of these assholes."

"Thank you so very much for that, brother," Inferno growled.

Ember just shrugged, stepping aside so Prince Blaze could also take her by the hand. He turned it over, bent low, and kissed it. "It's good to see you awake. Did you sleep well?"

The touch of his mouth didn't liquefy Fiona's insides the way Inferno's kisses did, but it still made her heat up. She couldn't speak when Prince Blaze lifted his eyes to grin at her, but when Inferno growled, Fiona realized this show was more to irritate his older brother than to be a traditional gentleman.

Fiona laughed nervously, pulling her hand back. "It's very nice to meet you. Thank you for letting me stay here."

Prince Blaze straightened. "Our pleasure. I hope you're feeling better after your ordeal."

"Introduce yourself, idiot," Ember hissed.

"What? Oh, right." Blaze cleared his throat, all the life leaving his eyes as a bored expression settled there. "I am the honorable Prince Blaze Blackclaw the Sixteenth, second in line for the dragon throne of the United Kingdom of Ameri—"

"Not like that, fool!" Ember snapped, smacking his brother over the back of the head, though there didn't seem to be much heat in it. "She's going to think we have metal rods up our asses."

"They'd be gold rods."

Ember rolled his eyes, shook his head, and stepped away.

Blaze chuckled at his brother, and while his previous introduction had all the spirit of a piece of cardboard, now his eyes positively danced, as if it excited him to see that he could annoy his sibling and that he was accepting a challenge to get it done.

Fiona blinked at the spectacle. She hadn't expected this, that was for sure. They were so casual, like real brothers, and nothing at all like the proper princes, or soldiers, she'd seen on TV or in magazines. They were bantering and fighting.

"Blaze, I adore you, but if you attempt to kiss my mate again, I might be forced to break your nose."

Blaze flipped him off as he lounged back in his chair. "Wouldn't be the first time, so whatever."

"I'm very sorry, but I still need to know what's going on," Fiona said, really hoping no noses got broken in front of her. "I think there's been a mistake. Inferno seems to think I'm his mate, and I need to tell him that he's got the wrong person."

She looked to both of Inferno's brothers, though she figured Ember might be the one who would have the most sympathy for her plight. There was no way Fiona could ever be the mate of a dragon prince. The odds of that were too much.

Ember sat down on the other side of the table, his back straight, unlike Blaze, who leaned back and kicked his feet up again.

"We're not sure there is a mistake," Ember replied.

Fiona blinked. "But I—"

"I know this is a lot for you," Inferno said, his voice sounding softer than before. Was he attempting to be calm and considerate here? "Come, please, have a seat. I will explain everything you need to know."

Fiona swallowed hard. Inferno pulled out a chair for her. She sat in it, allowing him to ease her closer to the table before he grabbed another seat and rolled it over so he was sitting next to her, the both of them at the head of the table.

Blaze took one of the tablets off the table, tapped something, and a projector slowly dropped from the ceiling just as the lights dimmed.

What it showed on the opposite white wall looked to be a couple of family trees that dated back centuries, coming to the present. Some of them were snuffed out in black.

She got the feeling she was supposed to be paying attention to the families that were blacked out, as if a cloud of smoke had just come in and stopped their progression, snuffing them out, and that this might have something to do with her.

Her and Inferno.

Inferno was the one to start. "What do you know about the Istavan family and the way dragons choose their mates?"

7

—————

Inferno watched her carefully, the way she blinked those wide green eyes up at what the projector displayed for her to see. How did it look to her? How did seeing those blacked out names, as if they had been charred by an unforgiving thick smoke of a poisonous fire, make her feel?

The Istavan family, which he was sure was hers, was blacked out. As was the Cesare family, which had been wiped out due to fighting, Bellemare, and Romulus, which had also been destroyed by the Capuletta family. Interesting story there. The Grimoult Family, Montgomery, Burns, Vis-De-Loup, and finally, the Fitzherbert family, which had also been destroyed.

Of the ten families, four had been thought to be wiped out through unnecessary battle and greed. Until now. Fiona was an Istavan.

Did she recognize what was up there? Even if it were just unconscious and instinctive, Inferno would take it. All the royal human houses seemed to know. It was always uncon-scious, but it was there, just as her lust and desire were. She denied it now, but the way she'd leaned back into him after pulling away from Blaze when the idiot had kissed her hand made it obvious.

"I..." she started, faltering, as though searching for the right words to use. "I've heard of some of these names. In magazines, or when the news talks about the dragon nobles, but I try not to pay too much attention to any of it. These are the families that can breed with dragons, right?"

Inferno nodded. "Yes. Exactly. Every generation or so, a new head of house in each noble dragon family find their mates within these families. For all of our recorded history, these families had produced strong, powerful dragons, and even some notable kings."

Fiona glanced at him before quickly looking away, her cheeks darkening. What had she thought just now for her to do that? Was she thinking of him? He hoped so.

Inferno continued. "This isn't always the case, however. Some dragons choose to breed with other dragons."

"Why do that?" Fiona asked, frowning at him. "That makes no sense. If your family and the noble dragons are mating with humans, then why fight it? I thought a dragon mating was supposed to be, you know, true love."

He could hear the hesitation and embarrassment in her voice, and Inferno was glad she'd asked this question.

"There are a couple of reasons this could happen," he started, rubbing the back of his neck. "Some have claimed they never had a natural-mating with the person in question from any of the human families you see on the wall. This is a possibility, given there's no reason anyone can think of as to why the dragon nobles would be drawn to these specific families to begin with."

Fiona looked down at her hands. "I always heard it was a romantic thing." She turned her gaze back up to him. "That these families were destined to be with each other, and that the dragon's true loves were within them."

Blaze chuckled. "It would be amazing if it was that easy."

Ember hissed at his brother. Inferno left them alone, his eyes only on his mate.

"That is a nice story to tell, but there are more political and survival aspects involved in all of it. These human families are the only ones we have on record that can bear dragon children. Natural-matings do happen, and they seem to occur frequently enough, though no one is sure if that's just a happy accident or not."

She looked away from him again, back at the bright image the projector cast. "You make it sound so dreary."

"So, what if it is?"

Inferno bit back a grunt when, in that next instant, he felt a rush of pain in his calf. He looked over. Ember glared back at him.

Ah, a signal to be more sensitive.

He'd get Ember back for that later. Right now, he needed to make things better with his mate. "It's not that bad. As I said, there are often natural-matings made with these pairings. It's to the point where we can, for the most part, predict which family will produce a mate for that generation. This time around, it was the Istavan family, but they were gone."

She didn't seem to catch that he meant her. "So, if there's not a natural-mating, what happens? One is just set up for you?"

"Pretty much. A union, a marriage. It might be devoid of instinctual-mating and simply done for the sake of a contract and reproduction."

"What if you want to make your own choice?" She looked from one brother to the next.

"Dragons who don't want to participate in their arranged

pairing choose a simple-mating with another dragon, which is frowned upon, or humans who could not bear them children, which is also frowned upon."

Fiona nodded, her face still bright from the light of the projector. "Right, you all don't like it when dragons mate other dragons because you almost consider it like marrying in the family."

"We do that sometimes, too," Blaze said, his allusion to Tinder and Inferno's engagement clear.

Inferno snapped his teeth at the man. If his brother wasn't on the other side of the table, he swore he might have leaped over it and smashed his head in.

"There is a higher chance the offspring will be weak and sickly, if not mediocre," Inferno explained.

"And what if a dragon doesn't choose the simple match with another dragon, or a regular human? What if they want to choose who to marry in the royal human lines?"

"Depending on the family of the dragon, the heir in question, and if there are siblings to take his place, some families can be lenient. Others are less forgiving."

"What do you mean?"

Inferno clenched his jaw. "You should not hear this now."

"I want to know. Tell me what that means."

Inferno steeled himself. She was a human and new to the concept of being around royalty, and she was his mate. Was this something he would have to get used to?

"Once, a dragon noble failed to find a natural mate with any of the families, so a mate was chosen for him — one of the Bellemares. The dragon, however, defied his parents and the contract, and chose a love match with a woman from the Cesare family instead. This would have had no negative consequences as he was still choosing from a line that would give him strong heirs, but after that, the entire Cesare family was destroyed. The Bellemares are suspected, but nothing could be proven."

If those eyes got any wider, she would look like a cartoon character. "What does this have to do with me?" Her voice was so tiny and quiet.

This was it. This was the question he'd been waiting for, and Inferno only ever felt this sort of excitement, this kind of adrenaline rush, when he was on the verge of flying into battle. He was eager, his body antsy to move, and more importantly, desperate to know what the reaction was going to be. Happiness? Sadness? Either way, he could experience it with her, and they could work through it together.

"Our families can usually predict who will be mated to whom based on the mating cycles. Some of the noble human families were wiped out for various reasons, fighting amongst each other for power being the main reason."

"Right, I know that. I heard it in school, but what does it have to do with me?" She paused. "Is it why those men came into my apartment and tried to kill me?" Her hand unconsciously climbed to her neck, as though making sure the flesh there was unharmed.

He ached for her just then but wishing he'd made it into that small apartment five minutes earlier to stop her horrifying ordeal would not magically make it so. He was a prince — not a god.

Fiona's eyes suddenly met his. He turned to point back at the projector before she would see something there he wasn't ready to reveal. "Do you see the Istavan family?"

Fiona looked. "Well, yes. It's gone, though."

"No, sweet. You are an Istavan princess. For all I know, their last surviving heir."

Fiona blinked, stared up at the image on the projector,

then looked at Inferno, before glancing back up at the projector, then to Inferno's brothers and back to him.

A loud giggle erupted as she shook her head. "No, that's a mistake. I'm not a missing royal."

"It's no mistake. This time around, it was estimated my mate would have been one of the Istavans. Because they were believed to have been wiped from the face of the earth, I would have married my cousin, Tinder. Then I found you in that bakery, wearing that ridiculous but cute little paper hat, and I felt it in my bones and blood."

She shook her head again. "No, I'm not. That's not...how could I be?"

Inferno didn't know what to tell her to make her believe this. He didn't understand her objection. Was it the shock of it? Or the title he'd given her? To be a princess was to be a fine thing, even amongst the humans who were barely royalty at all and only held those titles as part of their connections to the dragon noble families.

Ember, bless his fiery heart, was the diplomatic one, as usual. "We don't know how this happened, but Inferno saw you and realized who you were, and you seem to be reacting to him as well. It should also be said that the Istavan family was notable for having flame red hair and green eyes like yours."

This time, her hand went up to her hair. He wanted to reach out and touch it. He held back. She seemed too resistant to him for now, which was why he was taking it easy with her.

"But...how?"

"We don't know," Inferno admitted. "The last time an Istavan was meant to be mated to someone in my family, he eloped with a woman he'd been in love with and the family was never seen again. Over the years, and after much searching, it was assumed they had been killed off, which is why the names were blacked out."

Those green eyes shone suddenly bright. "My parents... they died. I was a little girl, but...did someone hurt them? Did someone kill my parents because of this?"

Inferno hadn't expected this, and the rush of protective instincts flared to life inside him once more.

"How did they die?"

Fiona rubbed just beneath her eyes, as though banishing tears before they had the chance to appear. "A car accident. I was a little girl at the time. Did someone intentionally hurt my parents?"

Inferno had to look away from those eyes, but only so he could gauge the reaction from his brothers. Blaze's eyes were wide. Ember seemed thoughtful, but in the end, both his brothers shook their heads, their suspicions aligning with Inferno's.

"I don't think so, sweet," he said.

"Are you sure?" She looked back at him, desperation swimming in her eyes. "How do you know?"

"I don't know, but I am guessing about this. You said you were a child. I think you were only attacked because of the way I was looking at you. It's unlikely that if anyone had tried harming you then that they would have failed for so long. I do not think you were under attack back then, but my promise remains," Inferno said, his insides blazing with the need to fight, to defend his mate, her honor. "I will find those responsible for your attack and I will see to it they suffer."

Fiona's shoulders sagged. She stared down at the table, refusing to look at anyone else.

Inferno sighed. "Turn the lights back on," he said.

Blaze tapped on the tablet. The lights gently brightened

as the projector turned off and was put away. Inferno stayed by the side of his mate. He couldn't bring himself to leave her, even if he knew he was not welcome to touch her.

"Do you promise?"

Inferno blinked. "Promise? To get your revenge?"

"Yes." Her eyes met his, blazing with life in a way he'd not seen on her before. She reached for him, gripped him by his leathers and held on tight with her small fists.

"You said you promised to get back at them, to make them suffer for what they tried to do to me. Look me in the eyes and say it. Swear on your life, or in blood. I don't care, but promise me again that you're going to find them and make them pay."

He held her gaze and didn't look away. "Where is this coming from?"

The glare that marred her brow was shocking, even as she looked away in an attempt to hide it. "They put their hands on me. They stuck that bag over my head and tried to kill me. Even if they weren't associated with my parents' death, I'm mad now. I'm fucking furious." She met his gaze again, that infuriated expression burning hotter than any fire a dragon could create. "Find them and get back at them for me and I'll never leave this place if that's what you want. I'll be your Istavan princess if that's what you want so badly."

The dragon within Inferno's body roared to life and spouted liquid fire around him. Anger and glee warred with each other inside him.

The corner of his mouth quirked up. "That's not exactly the way I would have wanted you to come to me, but to be sure, I will accept your terms and the challenge with it."

Fiona nodded, the fire still in her eyes, making her even

more of a beautiful goddess. He would take her right now if he could.

He would take her soon.

He took her wrists, removing her grip from his jacket. Her eyes widened, though she didn't pull away. "What are you doing?"

He turned her hand over and kissed the spot where his brother's lips had been, erasing them from her skin and putting his own there. The rush of tingling pleasure at the touch of his mouth to hers was almost too much for him to ignore, but for now, he must. "I'm letting you know my terms. I will one hundred percent protect you from harm, and find those who would see you hurt, but we won't be waiting until after I do before I make you mine."

He didn't need to do anything other than look at her face to know that she knew what he meant, and it was glorious. He was looking forward to the revenge he would bring for his mate, but he was also looking forward to that night.

8

Inferno could sense the tension within his mate as he walked her back to her room. Eric was still there. Of course, he would be. So were some other guards in the area who wouldn't need to be seen by Fiona, but they would be there, protecting her.

He nodded to Eric, who opened Fiona's door for her.

"Eric will be outside the door, as will many other guards," Inferno said. "If you need anything, you need only to ask, and a maid will be along shortly to see to you and help you dress."

Fiona's eyes widened. "You're not coming inside?" Her hand gripped his, and he felt her gentle tug on it, pulling him inside the room with her.

Inferno grinned, showing off the sharp points of his teeth. "Do you want me to?" He knew that wasn't what she meant, but just the idea that his mate could be hinting that she wanted him to come inside, to touch her, make love to her, was more than enough to make his wilder side burn with fire.

"I...well, yeah."

"That doesn't exactly sound confident." Inferno looked at her blushing face but felt the strength in her grip. He stepped through the doorway, and pulled the door closed, locking it but never taking his eyes away from the beautiful woman in front of him. She didn't turn her back to him either, though she did back up two steps. Inferno approached her. "Are you the sort of woman who enjoys it when her mind is made up for her?"

She blinked. "What?" Fiona stopped abruptly when the backs of her legs touched the bed she had been resting in barely an hour earlier.

Inferno didn't stop his approach. He leaned over her, forcing her back as he pressed his fists down on either side of her waist. "Do you like it when a man dominates you? Do you want me to decide when to take you? Or can you show any confidence in our arrangement?" He noted the way her throat worked as she swallowed. Fiona's lips were bright. She must have been biting them on the way back to her room when Inferno hadn't noticed.

And something occurred to him.

"Are you a virgin?"

The way her cheeks flamed up told him all he needed to know.

"You've never known a man's touch." It was a thrilling revelation. At the same time, it brought out all the protective feelings he felt for her and magnified them by a thousand.

"You would give me your virtue?"

Even for a prince, such a thing was still a tremendous gift.

He could hear the sudden rush of her heartbeat. Her green eyes dilated, and it was clear that his words, and the heat of his body so close, was having the proper effect.

She was anxious, but not fearful.

"You're eager," he said.

"And you're full of yourself."

Inferno chuckled. "That does tend to happen when you're born into royalty." He let his fingertips slide across her throat, gently touching the bruising that had been left behind from her attack.

Fiona shivered.

"Does it hurt to touch you?"

She shook her head, her chest heaving from their contact. "No."

"Do you want me to continue?"

She said nothing.

He continued to touch her, letting his fingers explore, then leaned in and pressed his lips to the bruising, brushing heat into her tender flesh.

She moaned. "That feels good."

Heat usually did feel good against bruised flesh. He did it again, pushing as much heat into her that he could without overheating her human skin.

She moaned again, reaching her hands up, threading her fingers through his brown hair, tangling it, messing it, and that was good because he wanted her to do whatever the fuck she wanted to him and he was going to let her. The heat of their mating was taking its hold on him, and he had been able to keep calm about it before, to prevent himself from showing the effects too much, but now that he was on top of her, could feel her body beneath the thin cotton pajamas she wore, smell her heat, and her sex, it was enough to make the dragon inside him react.

He was going to claim her, and he was going to do it now.

Inferno's fingers slid down to the elastic waist of her sleeping pants, and he pulled them slowly down...

Someone knocked on the door. Fiona moaned again when he pulled away, but it was a sound of disappointment.

Inferno clenched his jaw. "Yes?"

A softly spoken woman's voice answered. "My lord? I am here to give the lady her fitting."

"Who's that?" Fiona asked, her voice wonderfully breathless.

"Your maid," Inferno replied, and he couldn't very well be angry at the woman outside for doing her job. That would hardly be fair to her, though he couldn't quite bring himself to part from his mate just yet.

"Would you like me to return at a later time, my lord?"

"No," he called. "One moment." He looked back down at his mate, noting her flushed cheeks, her wild red hair spread out along the sheets beneath her. She was waiting to be taken, but for now, he was going to have to hold back. There were other matters to attend to.

"You're mine now."

Fiona bit her lips, then nodded. "You're mine, too."

Those words alone were enough to make the dragon inside him flare to life. Inferno had to push himself back before he sent the maid away after all.

"She will have clothing for you for the day. I will return to take you to eat and introduce you to the rest of the family. Maybe."

She blinked wide, sitting up when he was no longer on top of her. "Maybe?"

He smiled, taking her by the chin, leaning in, and capturing her lips. He pushed in another rush of heat, enjoying the sweet moan Fiona released when he did.

She was the first to pull back, shaking her head and covering her mouth with her hand. "How are you doing that?" Her eyes smiled as she looked up at him as if he was the most exciting person on the face of the earth.

"Dragon trade secret," Inferno replied. "I'll return shortly, I promise." He turned to go.

"Inferno."

He stopped, looking back.

Fiona's eyes were no longer playful, and though her red hair was messy and wild from their earlier actions, all other traces of lust were gone from her. "What if it was someone in those other human families who wanted to hurt me?"

He gave her his full attention. She continued.

"I mean, if I am from this family line, and these people have been fighting for years, I guess trying to get someone in their family to mate with whomever was next in line for the throne. If someone saw you on TV just looking at me the way you were, and they were able to figure it out from that alone—"

"Say no more, sweet, I've already thought of this," Inferno said.

He and his brothers had been speaking extensively about this since before Fiona had woken up, even before Inferno had gone to see his aunt and cousin. The fact that they were also on his list of suspects was something he was not ready to tell her yet, though Inferno had instructed Eric to let no one into Fiona's room that Inferno or his brothers hadn't already personally verified.

"My brothers and I will look into this. This attack on you will not stand, and Eric is loyal. Young, but loyal. You can trust him with your safety, and if you need anything from him, or if you feel frightened and I am not here, you can count on him to see to your needs, and he will send for me if he suspects anything."

Fiona nodded, though Inferno didn't think she realized

at that moment that she was picking at her fingernails. A nervous habit? Perhaps.

He didn't want to leave her like this, but there was no choice. He had to do some questioning of his own if he was going to allow his mate to walk these halls with any peace of mind.

"Does a prince usually get so involved in what the guards do? Or investigations like this?" Fiona asked.

Inferno smiled, putting one hand to his hip and rubbing his chin with the other. He didn't usually enjoy singing his praises when it came to matters such as this, but in this case, he thought it would be best.

"We are not like the humans you know of, your royalty or your nobility. The dragon royals have always fought alongside their warriors, and one cannot be a king without knowing how to sniff out and battle the enemy properly."

Fiona's brows lifted. "You're saying you're just as trained as the men around here are at protecting you?"

"Of course, ever since I was old enough to hold a blade or a gun." He wasn't so bad at hand-to-hand either. He'd made the top of his class several times over, and when in training with the other men around the palace itself, it wasn't unusual for him to best them in combat.

He didn't tell her that, however. There was reassuring her of his skills, and then there was bragging.

She seemed somewhat put at ease. "Do you think you could teach me how to defend myself? I mean, in case some-thing happens?"

He did not want her thinking she should have to go up against a group of men, or even a single man for that matter, but he had to admit, it might help if she could handle herself some.

"For your peace of mind, yes. We can start tomorrow if that is your wish. Hand-to-hand, and then the gun range."

The hand-to-hand would do nothing but teach her how to escape certain holds her attackers would have on her, and when and where to run. She wouldn't know how to fight off an actual attack properly. Not in the first lesson. Not even on the tenth. It took years to develop these skills.

The first rule of defending oneself was learning how to avoid the fight entirely. It was a lesson she would still need to learn.

Her smile, and the way her shoulders heaved, as though she had just launched a heavy weight from them, made his decision worth it.

"Your maid is waiting. I won't be long."

"Thank you. For everything."

He nodded. "For you, anything." The more he was around this woman, the more he was having trouble holding back. Typically, this was supposed to be the best time in a dragon's life with a natural-mate. But for now, Inferno had to hold back his instincts as much as he possibly could. He needed his head clear before he went back to his aunt and cousin to ascertain if they were perhaps involved in Fiona's attack.

Inferno hated to think about it like this, but since he was something of a betting man, he was willing to bet Tinder might be the one with the most significant motive to harm Fiona since she was the one Inferno would have married to replace the mate he never thought he would have. And she'd had a front-row seat to the fire that had ignited between the two at the bakery that day.

9

———

Inferno hadn't exactly been telling the truth. It wasn't just one maid. It was a trio of them.

The first woman, the one who had knocked on the door, had a timid appearance and voice but appeared to be the one in charge of the others. She gave a small curtsey to Fiona. "My lady, my name is Leanne. I will be honored to be your attendant."

Heat climbed right up into Fiona's face. Never in a million years had she imagined that someone would speak to her that way, especially while offering to perform tasks that Fiona personally hated. Her days working in a department store, folding clothes and finding different sizes for the customers to try on, had been some of the worst of her life.

"My lady?"

Fiona blinked. "Umm, sorry," she said, glancing over at the other maids who were in similar black skirts with white aprons. They had pulled in what appeared to be a small wardrobe on wheels. Many outfits were hanging from it. The other girl had a big cart with her, and when she settled it in the room and opened it, Fiona made out the many different bottles and containers of face washes, creams, scrubs, and other various bits of makeup.

None of them had any labels she recognized, but she was willing to bet they were all expensive.

"Is there something the matter, my lady?"

Fiona shook her head, though she felt as if she was having an out-of-body experience.

"I'm fine. I just...I'm not used to people talking to me like that."

Leanne blinked such a wide-eyed look it was almost owlish, but it still looked good on her.

"Ah, yes. I apologize. You're human, and were raised as a lesser."

"Lesser?"

"Non-royal," Leanne said, still smiling softly, innocently, as if she didn't realize how much she'd just insulted Fiona.

Fiona took in a deep breath and let it go. She was new here, so there was no point in getting worked up for nothing. "So there are more rules in the dragon world?" she asked.

"Nothing too specific, my lady," Leanne assured her. "This is simply for your station."

"My station?" Fiona asked, carefully watching the two women behind Leanne. They seemed to be quietly arguing over which set of clothes would be best for her to wear, what would go better with her hair, what would make her eyes stand out, and what piece would lift and accent her breasts the most. "Well, I could pick out something for myself. If that's okay." Fiona didn't want to seem too bossy if she was going to live here. These women were being hired to do a job, and it wasn't their fault that Fiona didn't want them to do it, but she was a grown woman, not a child, and certainly not a doll.

"I'm grateful you brought all these clothes here, and that you want to help me with them." Some of the clothes had back zippers, pantyhose, and other feminine-looking things that appeared she would need help with. She didn't even want to think about all that makeup. "But I don't need all of this."

Leanne frowned softly, glancing away from Fiona as if it would have been against the law to let someone else see her face when she was glaring. *Was* she glaring?

"Is that a bad thing?"

"No, my lady," Leanne said quickly. "It's just...rather uncommon from a lady from one of the high families to react in such a way. Apologies, I should not be saying so much."

"No, no, it's okay. I might need some of your help anyway. I just wasn't raised to need help with every single little thing. What, exactly, were you hoping to do to me?"

Leanne smiled at her this time, and at least now her expression was much more relaxed. "We will start with a wash. A bath with essential oils. We would very much like to pamper your hair. I know Fleur has never seen hair quite like yours before, and she is especially excited."

Fiona glanced to the side. Which of those two blushing maids was Fleur?

"Uh, well thank you. I appreciate the compliment." At least, she thought it was a compliment.

Growing up, Fiona had often been asked if she dyed her hair to look the way it did. Sometimes people didn't believe her when she claimed it was natural. Never once had she suspected it was the trait of a long lost noble family capable of mating and breeding with the dragons.

Fiona listened, almost in a daze, as Leanne went on and on about all the things they intended to do to her. She couldn't believe it. The more she heard, the more unbeliev-able it seemed. She'd thought she would just hop in the shower and come out to a fresh set of clothes. No. These women seemed as excited as school girls for Fiona to soak in a bathtub while they did treatments on her hair, face, and nails.

They wanted to give her a manicure, pedicure, and wax her whole body from the sound of it. Then massage some sort of skin scrub on her arms, legs, back, stomach, and even her breasts, before giving her a facial she'd never even heard of before. These ladies were looking less and less like maids in a dragon palace and more like they were supposed to be working in a spa somewhere.

"What do you think, my lady? Would this sound pleasant for you?"

"Uh, how long will all of that take?"

"With the three of us working together? Two hours if we hurry."

Fiona thought for one scary second that the floor dropped out from under her feet. "Two hours?"

All three women smiled at her as if they didn't see anything wrong with that time limit at all.

Inferno had said he'd wanted her to meet up with the rest of his family and show her around. He couldn't have meant for it to take that long for her to get dressed. Though, she had never had any spa treatment before, and she was insanely curious to try it out.

"How about I have a quick shower, and we can trim my hair later, skip the full body scrub, and just do the manicure, facial, and then I can pick out an outfit?"

From the looks she got, she might as well have offered to throw a kitten out the window.

"The waxing as well, though, yes?" Leanne asked.

Might as well go for it. "Sure, yeah. Though I should warn you, my legs are pretty gross right now."

Leanne smiled. "Ah, but remember it's a full body wax."

The tiny muscle beneath Fiona's eye twitched. "Uh, what else would you need to wax?" Her immediate thought went to her brows, but no sooner did she lift a hand to touch them did she remember there was hair on her arms as well, and then she knew what was going to happen.

One of the other maids, maybe Fleur, went to the trolly and rummaged through several small pots and bottles and rollers, and when one of the girls opened up a black case and revealed a swatch of colors, Fiona figured she might have bitten off more than she could chew, even after trying to portion this out.

Uh oh.

He found them in the gardens. His aunt, Princess Charrling, in a sundress and wide straw hat that hid away most of her sun-blonde hair. She was an older woman, sister to his father, but still beautiful. Her daughter, Lady Tinder, stood at her mother's side, arms held loosely behind her back as she spoke to her mother.

Their guards stood a reasonable distance away, enough to give the two women privacy, but close enough for their protection. Inferno nodded to one of the men as he passed.

He couldn't see the women's faces from this angle, but when he came around to the side and noted the redness and puffiness around Tinder's eyes, Inferno paused. Had she been crying? He'd expected it from her when there was room to make a scene, but crying alone with her mother wouldn't serve any selfish purposes. Perhaps it was the tears of someone who had just lost a game in the final round because theirs was undoubtedly never a love match.

He caught sight of a handkerchief in her hand, which she used to blow her nose. Shame crept into Inferno. Tinder couldn't have had anything to do with Fiona's attack. She might be spoiled, but she was a sheltered girl who didn't know how to drive a car on her own, let alone set up an attack on a woman. She wouldn't have noticed any spark between him and Fiona at the bakery, not when she'd been so focused on wedding plans.

Plans that he'd abruptly eliminated from her life with no hint of a warning.

He was so focused on getting the deed over with, breaking off the engagement, that he hadn't had the chance to consider her feelings and apologize. He figured that now something to that effect was going to have to be in order.

His aunt and his cousin attacking Fiona? Who until this morning was a virtually unknown lesser? No, that was unlikely, and now he felt like an ass for thinking it.

"Tinder?"

Tinder's red eyes flew wide as she looked up at him, then glared and turned her back. "What do you want?" Her voice was small and cracked as she spoke.

Charrling put her hands on her daughter's small shoulders. Her expression when she looked over Tinder's shoulder at Inferno was disappointed, though there was nothing there that hinted that she wanted to do him, or his mate, any harm.

"She needs some time, nephew."

The situation sucked. Sure, they'd promised to make each other happy, but here she was, left with nothing, while Inferno was entering into the best kind of life a dragon could hope for.

"Tinder, I just wanted to let you know that I'm sorry you're experiencing this unexpected and unfair treatment right now. None of us could have known this was going to happen when we first made our engagement. Nevertheless, you still have my protection, and I intend to do whatever I can to help you find a new match."

She didn't turn to face him. If anything, she appeared somewhat smaller at that moment as her shoulders bunched together. It was not good. Not good in the least.

If there was nothing he could do, he'd have to task Flare with comforting her. They didn't always get along, but they were family, and it was more ideal than letting someone waste away on the grounds. Maybe Flare could convince her to get back out there and find someone who would be a better fit than Inferno ever could have been.

Charrling looked down at her daughter, taking the younger woman by the cheeks so Tinder had to look up at her. Charrling smiled a warm, motherly smile as she whispered to Tinder in such a voice that even Inferno could not make it out.

Tinder nodded, then Charrling walked over to Inferno.

He stood straight, offering the older woman that respect.

"Can I have a word?"

Not what he expected.

"Of course."

With a parting glance at his cousin, he followed his aunt deeper into the rose garden.

It was a wide-open space. The humans seemed to think there should be a maze of shrubs in here, but that offered too much in the way of cover for potential assassins. No, there was a long fountain, stone paths that branched off, and very few garden bushes that were thick enough to hide behind. Even the rose bushes weren't allowed to become so tall or thick that they could provide much cover.

Because of this, even when they were fifty feet away from Tinder, Inferno could still see her in the distance as she sat dejectedly on a bench.

Charrling sighed. "Well, there is nothing to be done for it if you're certain the woman is your natural-mate."

"I am," Inferno replied. "I'm also more than willing to help with Tinder however I can."

Charrling scoffed. "The Crown Prince rejecting her will look bad on her prospects for a noble match. Though, because of her connections to you and the family, I have been trying to explain that things are not so bleak. Regardless, tongues will wag for the rest of her life."

Inferno sighed, running his hand through his hair while propping the other on his hip.

"Why do our mating habits need to be so complicated?"

Charrling huffed a small laugh. "Well, at least we have them. The humans have been making a mess of it since they stopped climbing around in their trees and left their caves. They forgot their instincts." She looked at Inferno again, her blue eyes flashing with a harsh glow. "You are quite certain?"

He knew what she meant. "I am."

"Because when the families were looked at, the Istavan family would have produced a mate for you this time around."

"And they did."

Charrling narrowed her eyes.

"She is an Istavan. I knew it the instant I saw her. I felt it."

"How very unexpected."

More and more he was beginning to sense a hidden layer of displeasure that made his hackles rise. "She will be my queen, and there is an investigation into who could have sent those men to her apartment. Blaze filled you in on that incident?"

She faced Tinder, but she gave him a sideways glance. He'd seen that look on her face before when he'd been a child and had been misbehaving. He was going to have more of a problem here than he'd thought, but not because they had something to do with Fiona's attack. This was something else he didn't entirely understand, but he was going to have to deal with it. Because at some point, he'd have to introduce Fiona to these two women, and there was likely nothing he could do to get his aunt and cousin to like it.

"How long can I expect the two of you to be out of commission, from social events and—*gah!*" Inferno stopped short when he felt something hard smack him on the back of the head. He turned. Ember was there, glaring at him with his full set of teeth bared.

When had he gotten there?

"Idiot," Ember hissed, smoothening out his expression to something more pleasant when he faced their aunt. "Charrling."

She nodded. "Ember."

Inferno rubbed the back of his head. "Did you just punch me?"

"Only before you could make yourself look like more of an idiot. How is Tinder?"

Charrling glanced toward her daughter. "Young, fearful of what everyone will think, and unsure of what her future will hold, but with some effort, she will recover."

Inferno could understand Tinder's pain and would extend his compassion to her. He was more impatient with Charrling's attitude, though. She has the same wisdom of other dragons her age and should understand better than most the intricacies of dragon mating. Best to not ask about it, however. If Ember was willing to hit him over it, then it must have been an *insensitive* question, as Ember and Blaze would put it.

He didn't get the chance to ask about anything else before his watch suddenly vibrated. He and Ember glanced down, having the same device on their wrists. They looked at each other, a silent agreement stretching between them as Inferno started to run.

The silent alarm had been tripped. Ember would stay with the ladies. Inferno needed to get back to his mate.

10

———

"**I**s something going on?"

Fiona noted the way the maids had all looked down at their wrists at what appeared to be incredibly high tech watches. She went on high alert after observing the distress on their faces.

When they didn't answer her, Fiona stood up, not caring about the wax strips on her legs, or that her face was half covered in a green mask of some sort.

"What's going on?"

The bedroom door burst open. Fiona jumped slightly just as Eric and three other men in black suits and sunglasses stormed inside.

Okay, guards with guns didn't do that sort of thing if there was no reason for it. Eric went to the windows, pulling shut the curtains that Fiona had only managed to get open because she didn't want to feel so closed up. More men stood guard at the door.

That just made her all the more nervous. "What's going on? What's happening?"

"It's just a precaution," Eric said, smiling softly, and

almost managing to look normal for her with his sunglasses and earpiece. "An alarm went off. You're Lord Inferno's top priority, so we will stay in here until given orders to leave."

Fiona figured that made sense, but as she looked around, she couldn't help but wonder. "Isn't this a bit much for just an alarm?"

She tightened her bathrobe around herself. She wasn't about to let a wardrobe malfunction happen around a bunch of guys she didn't know. It was bad enough they could see her hairy, half waxed legs, and the part of her face that had the green stuff on it was starting to tingle and burn.

She reached back for a cloth to wipe at her face.

"My lady, don't smear it," Leanne said, but it was too late. She was getting it off her face.

"It burns too much," Fiona said. And she looked ridiculous. "I think I'm allergic to it."

She went to a mirror as she wiped it off her cheek and forehead, to make sure she got all of it. It was starting to burn even worse now. Maybe she should have done this with a damp cloth.

When she saw herself in the mirror, Fiona was suddenly glad that the alarm did go off, because if what he was seeing was real, then there was no way in hell she wanted this stuff on any part of her skin.

She pulled back, faced Eric, and pointed at herself. "Am I seeing this right?"

Even with the sunglasses on, the way his mouth tightened was obvious. The other men in the room appeared to be trying to not look at her at all, as if they were hoping Fiona wouldn't ask them such an awkward question. Half of her face was bright red. Bright red and still burning.

"Oh God," she said. "Do you have anything for this?"

Leanne's hands were at her mouth. She appeared almost

in shock before she finally snapped out of it and pulled something off the tray of potions and waxes. It looked to be a wipe of some sort.

"Here, my lady, come. I will fix this."

"Ow," Fiona said when Leanne touched her face. She wasn't rough, and whatever that little cloth was made out of was as smooth and soft as could be. It was almost like a baby wipe that had been dipped in essential oils. The problem was how much the simplest touch was making the burn feel that much worse.

"I don't know what happened. This was not supposed to happen." Leanne went on and on with her apologies. Fiona didn't know what to say to her. She'd always had sensitive skin, but she'd never had a reaction like this before.

"I guess it's a good thing the alarm went off, ow," Fiona said, trying to make light of the situation, but still wincing as Leanne tenderly wiped down her face. She eventually switched to a new wipe, and this time, Fiona almost felt something akin to relief, but then the worry settled in.

"Is it nasty?"

What if her face stayed bright red for several days? What if her face started to peel, or swell up? What would Inferno say when he looked at her then? Surely, he wouldn't think she was so good to look at when she resembled something that could have landed from Mars.

A soft, helpless noise escaped her throat before she could stop it.

Leanne kept babbling. "I will fix it, my lady. I promise you. I am so sorry; the green tea mask wasn't supposed to do this."

As if to confirm all of her nightmares, Inferno's voice could be heard booming down the hall, and the amazing thing was that he didn't even sound angry.

"Where is she? Is she all right?"

Damn, his voice could carry.

And he was going to walk in here and see her looking like this any second now.

The idea of that made her panic a hundred times more than the way her face looked or the suspicious way all the guards had just swarmed into her room.

"Leanne, he can't see me right now."

Leanne nodded. "Of course. Here, keep this on your face."

Leanne handed her that nice soft cloth she'd been using, and even though the mask had been a disaster, this thing had been touching her skin enough that she was reasonably confident she wasn't going to get her face burned off from it.

She held it completely over her face while Leanne went to the door just as Inferno walked in.

God, she was still wearing this fluffy bathrobe with wax on her legs. This was a nightmare.

"Fiona?" Inferno called.

She didn't look at him.

"The lady is fine, my lord," Leanne said. "A mishap with the facial."

"Mishap?" he asked, his voice sounding much closer.

He was coming towards her.

Fiona stepped away and walked right into the tray that had been holding all the waxes and cosmetics. She might have knocked it over had a pair of small hands not grabbed her by the shoulders. Likely it was Fleur, or the other maid.

"Fiona, let me see."

"No, I'm all right." She didn't dare take her face out of the cloth. No way. No way in hell was she going to let him see her looking as red as a stop light. It was almost as bad as finding out her boss had taken credit for her recipes. She was not going to let a handsome dragon prince see her looking like this. Worse still when it was a handsome prince she wanted to throw herself at just because he was in the same room.

Fuck, that mating heat thing, whatever it was, was already pulling her to him. She couldn't take that. Not now.

"Fiona, it's all right. It can't be that bad."

"It's that bad, and you're not going to see it." She hoped the tone of her voice made it clear how serious she was. She also wanted to take some of the attention off her, though she wasn't sure how successful she was, considering she was still holding a baby wipe to her face with both hands. "What was happening with the alarm? Was it dangerous?"

"No, a couple of reporters and photographers tried sneaking onto the property. They haven't tried that in a while."

Did that mean some people knew she was here? Did the public know Fiona was in this castle? Did they know why?

She needed to get online as soon as possible.

"The rest of you can return to your posts," Inferno said.

Fiona heard the guards silently walk out of the room, and though she was glad they were gone, the tension in her shoulders didn't lessen with Inferno there, watching her.

"Are you certain you don't want me to see? Whatever it is cannot be that bad."

Typical guy. He didn't get it.

Thank God Leanne was there to talk some sense into the man.

She kept her voice low, though Fiona could still hear everything she said. "My lord, women can be sensitive about these things. Please, leave this matter to me, and I will see to it that she is well cared for."

"Will she be well enough for dinner tonight?"

Dinner? Right, with his family. But there was also something else they were supposed to be doing tonight, something that just thinking about made her stomach clench and her blood warm.

"I might need to stay in here tonight. Alone."

The sudden silence in the large bedroom was incredibly noticeable.

"Let me see your face."

"Nope." She walked another couple of feet, out of the hands of the woman who had been holding her steady. Of course, she banged her knees into something else that was hard and painful. Probably the leg of a table or a chair. Fiona hissed when she felt part of her skin that still wax on and no strip touch the object, and then pull stickily away.

She was making a mess of everything.

"It cannot be that bad, and you will still have dinner tonight with the rest of the family."

"Can we cancel it?" There was no way the red on her face was going to go down enough for her to have dinner with royalty.

"No."

Fiona didn't expect the hard edge to his voice. She didn't like it either. She pulled the cloth away from the part of her face that wasn't hot and burning while keeping it pressed to the side that was. She had to look at him if she was going to glare at him.

He glared back at her, his arms crossed.

"I can't go to dinner tonight."

"You will be fine. It's just with family. No photos will be taken of you, and there will be no press or nobles there to judge you."

"Will your ex-fiancée be there?" Fiona didn't think she could handle having dinner and pretending everything was all right around the woman whose man she stole. Was it still stealing if it turned out Fiona was his true mate? Well, she didn't know, and she didn't want to take the risk of rubbing it in. It would just be worse if Fiona looked like a cherry tomato.

"She will have to be there. She is my cousin and part of the family."

"Then I can't do it."

"She will understand. You will have to meet her eventually. Stop acting petulant."

Fiona snapped. She couldn't hold it in. "Well stop treating me like this is supposed to be normal!" In her anger, she threw the cloth covering her face to the floor.

Inferno's eyes widened, and he finally, finally looked like he wasn't in complete command of everything.

"Someone tried to kill me last night! They broke into my apartment and tried to strangle me, and you kidnapped me and brought me into another country without my permission. Now you think I'm going to mate with you and be with you and have dinner with your family without any thought of what my needs might be right now?"

Even now she was struggling with the heat that was intensifying in her body. It was as if someone turned up the thermostat by several degrees, and she had no idea what she was supposed to do about that because this was crazy.

It was crazy that every time she looked at Inferno, she saw him naked. It was crazier still that she thought about all the stuff she wanted to do to him when she did get his clothes off.

Inferno clenched his hands into fists, growling through his teeth, "I am keeping you here for your protection."

"Yeah? And how well is that going when reporters can sneak onto your property whenever they want?"

Leanne suddenly spoke up. "Fleur, Anne, out, right now."

"Leanne, don't go." Fiona didn't want to risk what would happen if she was alone with Inferno. Her body trembled from all the yelling, but not only that, she was terrified that she was going to jump into his arms and have make up sex with him.

"What's wrong with you? Tell me right now."

She nearly flew off the handle. "*What's wrong with me?*"

"Your *face*," he clarified. "You look as if you're in pain."

She was in pain. The swelling was setting in. She could feel it beneath the cloth. Her other eye wasn't quite swelling shut, but it was almost there. "I'm having an allergic reaction to one of the facials," she admitted miserably. This was not any fun, and she didn't want him to see her like this.

Inferno stepped forward again. Fiona backed off, but he was faster, reaching out and snatching her by the wrist before she could get away. "You will not run and hide from me."

The breath was swept out of Fiona's lungs as she stared up into his determined gaze. He loomed over her, so big and strong. The skin-to-skin touch of his hand on her wrist was enough to make her pulse skip. At that moment, the only thing Fiona could focus on was Inferno's bottom lip. She saw its color, its shape. She also saw herself biting down on it.

It was just the two of them in the room. In the world. There was no one else but them.

And Leanne. "I should go."

"Stay," Inferno said, and when he lifted his hand to turn her chin and examine her face, she was helpless to stop him. She was too transfixed, like an animal being hypnotized by its prey.

Inferno frowned softly, letting his hand come up, his fingertips gently touching her swollen cheek. Even though he barely grazed her, Fiona hissed. "An allergic reaction did this?"

"Yes, my lord," Leanne said.

Inferno's jaw tightened. "Show me."

He broke eye contact with her, and just like that, the spell was broken, and Fiona could breathe again. Holy God, that was intense. What the hell was that? Her wrist was tingling where Inferno was still holding onto her, but it was nothing at all like the burning on her face.

Fiona barely noticed as Leanne showed Inferno the pot of facial cream that was supposed to set on her face.

"How long was it on for?"

"Just a moment, my lord. We didn't have the chance to put the rest on because our alarms went off."

So that was why they'd been looking at their watches.

Inferno released her wrist. Fiona felt cold without him holding onto her, but he picked up the pot of green face cream and examined it. What was he looking for?

"My lord?" Leanne asked.

"What is it?" Fiona wanted to know, too.

The lips that Fiona had been thinking about biting and kissing hardened before he looked back to Leanne. "You've used products that are too harsh on her. We'll need to replace all of this."

He was serious, too. Inferno took the beauty cart by the handle and wheeled it towards the door.

That only made Fiona even more alarmed. "Where are you going?"

"I'll see you at dinner tonight," he said, still glowering as he left the bedroom.

11

Inferno was careful as he held onto the pot of green goo.

He loved women. He adored them. He was never going to understand all the things they did to themselves, however — lotions and creams for their entire bodies, not just their faces. Tinder had set aside two days out of the week to go and sit in a room for an hour at a time with what she'd called an oatmeal mask on her face while getting her nails done and cuticles cut.

Inferno swore he would never have known what cuticles were had it not been for polite society and the women he had to socialize with. Then there were the cases and cases of colors they carried around with their nail polishes and eye shadows. Body scrubs that had actual sparkles in them. It all seemed like such an effort to do something that didn't produce many results. Inferno never noticed a difference in any of the women he'd dated before committing to the marriage between himself and his cousin.

Inferno brought the mask to Ember's apartments. He needed his brother for this.

He nodded to the guards in black standing outside the door to the office. None of the private chambers in the palace would ever be without protection.

The door was opened for him, and he let himself in. Ember wasn't there.

"Call my brother for me," Inferno commanded, setting the pot onto the table in the middle of the room. It was still warm from being heated, and now there was a strange odor to it.

"Yes, my lord."

The guard shut the door behind him, and Inferno waited for his brother to come to him. Ember was good with these sorts of situations. Even now, Inferno struggled with himself to hold back his temper. He wanted to find out who was responsible for this and put them in a world of pain.

That was a simple reaction based on nothing but anger and rage—not exactly a regal reaction. Sometimes, a king needed to work silently, swiftly, and intelligently if he was going to get the results he wanted.

He was sure there was something off about what was inside this pot, but how was he to know for sure until the proper tests could be done? Even with his influence, it could take days, possibly weeks, before the results came back.

Inferno glanced up at the vase of fresh flowers in the middle of the table. Neither he nor any of his brothers were much into greenery, but the staff put them out because they looked elegant and added a fresh scent to the rooms.

Also, it was tradition.

Inferno reached out and took one of the roses by the stem. It was a fat bud; it had yet to open and bloom. He turned it upside down and placed it into the concoction on the table.

Leanne and Fiona had said the mix had only been on

her face for a minute, possibly less than that. He watched the bud in the mixture, and although it didn't hiss, bubble, or smoke, his instincts told him that this experiment would be telling.

The door behind Inferno opened, heavy footsteps walking up behind him. "You summoned me, brother?" Ember's tone was hardly serious, but Inferno hadn't exactly told the guard what he was calling Ember for.

"What do you make of this?"

"Make of what?" Ember came to stand beside Inferno. "What are you doing?"

Inferno pulled the rose out of the green mixture. He looked at his brother, then reached out and pulled the embroidered handkerchief out of his pocket, using it to wipe off the goo as gently as possible.

"Is there something important about this?"

"This was the cream, face mask, whatever it was, that was being put onto Fiona's face. I had it in there for about two minutes before you showed up."

He also couldn't wipe away the green stuff without ripping apart the petals beneath. It was hard to tell because of the mixture, but the red rose had browned and shriveled, burning under the influence of the mask.

Ember noticed it as well. "That was going to be put on the face of your woman?"

Inferno slammed his fist onto the table. "It *was* put on her face," he growled through his teeth. He shoved the pot of goo at his brother. "You have connections and know who to ask. Take this and get it tested. Someone in the palace is trying to harm Fiona."

And another horrifying thought occurred to him.

What if the same person in the palace was the person who had sent those men after her in her apartment last night? Inferno could have brought her directly into danger instead of away from it.

It was clear Fiona wasn't going to have her spa treatment finished today since Inferno had handed off the beauty cart to one of the guards, who had whisked it away. Leanne finished waxing her legs, but Fiona had to wash off all the excess bits of wax left behind on her own.

"Isn't he being a little overprotective?"

"Just precautions, my lady," Eric said with a smile that couldn't have been faker if he'd tried. "This is something of an annoyance for the lords and ladies of the household, but if there is ever an episode like the one you just had, an allergy, or a small accident, then it's policy to take all the materials and have them examined."

"Oh." She still wasn't sure she believed him, not with the way Inferno had walked out. Fleur still looked kind of irritated that her routine was being interrupted.

"What about these? Can I keep using these?" Fiona held up the pack of baby wipes she was using to soothe her face.

Eric got that uncomfortable expression back on his face. He was going to need a bigger pair of shades. If those things were made to hide the feelings of the men who wore them, making them look sinister and whatnot, then, at least for Eric, they weren't doing a very good job.

"Well, are they making you feel better? They're not irritating your face?"

"No, it feels a bit better." The swelling in her eye and cheek didn't seem to be getting any worse. Fiona hoped that it would go down enough in time for this dinner she was expected to have with Inferno's family.

Even though she'd already met his brothers, and was sure they would be kind to her, she still didn't want to show her face like this. And she would have already been nervous about meeting Tinder with a healthy face, but how was she supposed to show up like this?

Eric turned away from her, putting his hand to his ear and muttering something with his head down. There was a pause, some more muttering, another pause, and then he returned his attention to her. "You should be all right so long as you don't feel any more adverse effects."

Fiona blinked at him. "Did you just call Inferno and *ask* him if I could keep using these?"

Eric straightened his spine. "He is the lord of the house, my lady."

Unbelievable, but what the hell was she supposed to say against the prince of dragons? Giving Eric shit seemed kind of mean, too. He was only doing his job.

"Can we get some backup makeup in here? I'd like to at least put on some foundation to cover it up."

"We had such plans," Leanne moaned. The older woman was wringing her hands as if this entire thing was too stressful for her to handle. "We were going to do hair and makeup."

Eric nodded. "I'm sorry for the delays, but you will get everything you need. New products have been sent for. They should be arriving shortly."

"New products?" Fiona didn't understand. "Ones I won't be allergic to?"

"I'm sure they've reviewed the ingredient list and narrowed down the culprit. Everything they're sending up will be sealed and unopened and fine for you to use, my lady," Eric said, and Fiona noticed the emphasis on sealed and unopened.

Fine by her. Brand new makeup sounded pretty good. "Well, thank you so much then," she said, feeling kind of bad for being so fussy. Her face was burned, but that was no one's fault. She was allergic to something, and not only was that an accident, but Inferno was making it up to her by having his employees go out and find her products that would be more sensitive for her skin. Maybe the regular products the maids used on dragon skin had just been too harsh for hers.

She was starting to get just a little bit uncomfortable with how many more men in black were standing around her room. There seemed to be a lot more than there had been a few minutes ago. Weren't they all supposed to be outside?

They were likely standing in whatever post they thought Inferno would like them to be in. Surely the last thing anyone wanted to do was have his wrath targeted at them. She'd have to take control of the situation herself if she didn't want to be overwhelmed with guards at all times.

"I need some of you to clear out. Please." The guards looked to Eric, who opened his mouth to say something before Fiona cut him off. "We don't need that many bodies inside my private quarters. Inferno said they took care of the reporters who snuck in, and there aren't any rogue cosmetics in here ready to jump on me. I think we're fine."

A look of surprise hit Eric's face, and then he smiled a little. Fiona could tell he was impressed that she could give directions. He signaled for the guards to file out into the hallway, and Fiona chuckled.

"Well done, my lady" Leanne looked at her in wonder.

"That was nothing. You should see my ability to wrangle crowds flooding into the bakery 30 minutes before close on

Sunday. They'd kill each other over the on-sale leftover cupcakes if I didn't know how to get them in line!"

Just then, a woman Fiona had never seen before bounded into her room, practically dancing on the high-heeled toes of her knee-high boots, mall bags in hand.

A lot of bags.

"I'm *here!*" she sang, as the three maids rushed to relieve her of all the gear she'd hauled in.

Fiona was completely tense. Who was this woman? She wasn't Tinder, as Fiona had met Tinder at the bakery, and knew what she looked like from all the tabloids. This new woman seemed completely comfortable waltzing in past Fiona's guards, and before she closed the door behind her, she lowered her heart-shaped sunglasses and locked eyes with one in particular. "Eric," she said in a voice much lower than the one she'd used a moment before.

Eric pressed his lips together and didn't return the greeting, which caused the woman to laugh, and then shut the door, leaving just the women inside.

The woman's hair was something else. It was so full of body that it flew around her head, as though it was alive on its own. It was the prettiest shade of brown Fiona had ever seen, with a soft golden brown base streaked with darker chestnut with slashes of red that seemed to glow under the light of every lamp in the room.

Fiona was kind of jealous.

The woman took off her French-styled black cap, tossing it aside before undoing her red silken scarf, which was meant more for style than for warmth. And her red-brown eyes sparkled down at Fiona as if she was the most exciting thing on the face of the earth.

"So, you're going to be my new sister-in-law."

Fiona frowned briefly right before both her eyes flew wide, recognition finally dawning on her. "Princess Flare?"

"In the flesh! God, I love your hair. It's naturally like that? They always said the Istavans had amazingly red hair. I tried going with the streaks, too, but mine aren't natural like yours." Flare walked right up to Fiona and touched her hair, pulling it up and then dropping it down, so the strands fell like a red waterfall around her.

Fiona stood dumbstruck. She couldn't believe she didn't recognize the princess, but in all fairness, Flare had become a master at avoiding the paparazzi and staying out of the spotlight in recent years.

"Sorry, was it because I mentioned the Istavans? Does it bother you?"

Now she thought Fiona was suddenly shy over the mention of her dead family. Fiona shook her head. "No, I'm good. I'm just a little nervous about meeting you. I didn't recognize you at first."

"That's the idea," Flare said, suddenly smiling again. "My brothers go to events and get their pictures taken more than I do, especially Inferno since he's the heir. I can still go out. Chances are someone will recognize me, but there won't always be press lurking around with cameras, you know?"

"No," Fiona said, feeling suddenly helpless against this woman's good mood.

"Well, you're going to know it soon enough. Being mated to Inferno is one thing, but also being a long lost Istavan? The public is going to want to know all about you. I've been dying to meet you ever since I found out. I feel bad for Tinder, but she'll get over it. Just between you and me, I think she was more interested in the fame and attention than actually taking on any royal duties."

"You don't say." Fiona knew the rumors that had been published about Tinder said just that, but she wasn't about to start gossiping. She didn't want to get that kind of reputation.

"Anyway, it's time to work some magic. I brought stuff for face, hair, and makeup." Flare regarded her for a moment. "Cheer up, buttercup! This will be fun."

"I'm sorry, I just feel bad, that they sent you out to get all of this for me—"

"Stop right there!" Flare cut her off and sat down on the bed next to her. "I'll take any excuse for shopping, and I mean any, but being able to do something for my new sister is a gift. Do you know how often my brothers leave me out of things? This just gave me a chance to wheedle my way in here."

"Well, thank you," Fiona said, swallowing the word "sister." She'd never had a sister before, but always thought it might be nice to have someone who would have your back for life.

Flare grabbed Fiona's free hand. "Let's not waste any more time getting you ready then." She looked down, "Ah yes, I brought stuff for nails too."

Fiona felt her cheeks heat as the princess looked at her stubby fingernails. Flare's nails were done up in a pretty French manicure, but being a baker meant there wasn't often the chance for Fiona to indulge in getting her nails done. Now she was about to get them done with a real dragon princess sitting beside her, as eager and full of energy as if they were little girls about to do their braids together and make friendship bracelets.

"What do you think?" Flare asked.

Fiona swallowed hard. "Well, if you can promise me one thing."

Flare's smile became brighter, something Fiona hadn't thought possible. "Sure thing."

That smile melted away when Fiona revealed the messier side to her face. "Do you think we'll be able to could cover this up?"

Flare's unblinking expression, the way she stared in seriousness at the redness and swelling on Fiona's face, didn't bode well for her.

But the princess put on a determined smile and cleared her throat. "We're sure as hell going to do it, and I guarantee you will have a very grand first entrance."

Okay, Fiona didn't believe that, but she appreciated the enthusiasm, and decided that she already liked Inferno's sister.

12

Flare and Fiona walked through the palace, arms linked, while Flare chatted away about anything and everything she could. Fiona couldn't get over how normal Flare acted, as if wandering through a palace full of men with guns, while wearing Gucci heels and Ralph Lauren sundresses, was nothing out of the ordinary. The fact that it *was* normal to this woman boggled Fiona's mind, and she couldn't even start to wrap her head around the idea that this was supposed to be her new reality. She wore clothes that would pay a year's worth of her rent while chatting it up with a princess, and this wasn't a dream; this was reality.

Eric and a few of the other palace guards followed behind at a distance. So far, everything seemed quiet, and her time with Flare had almost helped her to forget all of the drama of the past 24 hours.

Fiona nodded and smiled at Flare, who was talking about her cute watercolor instructor, and how it annoyed her brothers that she spent her time on men like that. Fiona wished she could completely lose herself in the light chatter with Flare, but too much was going on for her to forget all of her cares and worries completely.

She had her life ripped away from her. Sure, it wasn't as nice a life as this, but it had been hers. Now, she was the mate of a dragon prince, the *heir*, and didn't even fully know what that meant. What duties would they expect of her?

And how on earth was she supposed to face Tinder?

At least Flare and her maids combined had been able to work some magic with makeup on the angry side of her face. The redness and swelling was unnoticeable. Almost. The skin was still hot, and there was some discoloration, but she looked a thousand times better now than she had before.

"Are you okay? Fiona?"

Fiona blinked, looking at the other young woman, realizing that she'd stopped walking.

Shit.

"Yeah, sorry. I guess I just got lost in my head there for a second."

Flare's smile was no longer quite so dazzling or bright. There was something softer in her eyes, and Fiona recognized it as sympathy.

"Sorry. I know I'm talking a lot. I was trying to take your mind off of everything. If it's bothering you, I'll stop."

"Of course you're not bothering me. There's just a lot going on, and it's a little hard for me to focus right now."

"It's one thing to join with your mate, but I guess it's a whole other thing when you didn't even know you were in the running," Flare said, smiling brightly again, as though trying to lighten the mood.

Fiona smiled. "That's true." She got serious. This was her chance to ask before it was too late and she was facing

Tinder at dinner. "About Inferno's, uh, ex? Can I ask you about her?"

"Oh, right, well don't worry about it too much when we get to the dining room. She probably won't look at you, will leave early, and you might not see her until the official ceremony for your wedding."

Holy shit. Fiona hadn't even thought about a proper wedding.

She'd seen the old footage of Inferno's parents being united on YouTube, so she had some idea of what to expect. She just didn't know how she was going to deal with planning an event like that on top of everything else that she was trying to get a handle on right then.

"So, wait, do we have to wait to have sex till then?"

Flare cringed. "It's really weird talking about my brother's sex life."

"Sorry," Fiona said, though she wasn't actually. She just wanted to know what to expect, how long she'd have to deal with the burning for Inferno before they could act on those feelings.

"It's okay, uh, well, you're probably going to end up sleeping with him before the actual ceremony. It's not like dragons are strict about being chaste or anything. The wedding is just a big party that's part family celebration and part show, so the world can see that the royal dragon has officially chosen a mate. But since you're his natural mate, you're pretty much his wife right now."

Fiona's throat dried up instantly. "Right now?"

"Yeah, natural mates are bonded from the moment they meet," Flare said, patting Fiona's newly-manicured hand, and continuing with their walk. "The mating will call the both of you to each other the more you're around each other. You're probably going to be with him after the dinner." Flare bit her lips together, clenching her eyes shut and shaking her head as if the whole topic was painful to talk about. "I really don't want to think about my brother having sex. Do you have any more questions, or can we move on to a new topic?"

"Yes, we can move on. Thank you, though, for helping me know what to expect." Fiona was happy letting Flare's thoughts move on to other topics, but her mind stayed stuck on Inferno. The panic about dinner was there, but even stronger was her desire to get through the meal so she could be alone with Inferno. She'd never been with a man, but every fiber of her body wanted to pull him into her room and lock the doors and the windows so the rest of the world and all her worries would stay out while she focused on just him. She didn't want to learn any more about mating, or wonder who attacked her or fret over Tinder's reaction. She wanted to bask in these feelings that she had for him, wanted to let him ignite her with every touch, and wanted to see what amazing things they could do together.

Okay, maybe she'd have to work harder to stay focused on idle chatter with Flare, least her heated body give away her thoughts.

They turned down what Fiona thought would be another long corridor with vast halls and tall ceilings, but no, the double mahogany doors were just being held open. This was a room, not another hallway.

There were vases of flowers placed along several spots on the long table, as well as in the corners to add some color to the room. Not that it needed much color considering the artwork on the walls and the crystal chandeliers that made the place seem to glow like in a fairytale or a dream. Fiona marveled at it for a second. If she were an artist, she would want to paint this room and all the colors in it.

A place like this didn't give the impression that dragon shifters lived here, that was for sure. The only indication she was still in the palace, and not in a painting, were the guards who were already standing at attention around the corners of the dining room. Fiona thought they looked familiar, but all the faces of these guys were starting to meld together.

A woman cleared her throat in a tiny, nearly coughing noise.

Fiona snapped her attention back, her eyes flying wide at the sight of two women sitting at the elegant dining room table.

She almost hadn't noticed them even with their wide-brimmed hats. They'd practically blended in with the rest of the room in the flower-patterned sundresses they wore.

Flare seemed to stand a little straighter, holding Fiona's hand a little tighter. "Aunt Charrling, Tinder, this is Fiona, Inferno's mate."

Even Flare's voice seemed to crackle a little at that last bit, as if she knew it was something of a cruel thing to introduce another woman as Inferno's mate when the man's ex was sitting right there.

Fiona had seen these women on the occasional magazine and in television. Tinder's face had been shown more, the world advertising her as the future Queen of Dragons. Princess Charrling only seemed to get some magazine space or television time whenever she was spotted out shopping with her daughter for wedding items.

She could hardly move as the two women observed her. Princess Charrling was the first to smile, and while there was nothing about her expression that warned of any hostility, Fiona couldn't help but shiver from the cold of it.

"It's a pleasure to make your acquaintance, dear. Please don't be shy. Come on over here so I may get a look at you."

The older princess pushed her chair out, though she didn't rise to her feet.

Fiona didn't know what to do, and it seemed rude for her not to do what a princess told her to, so she stepped away from the relative safety offered by Flare and towards the older woman.

Princess Charrling delicately reached her gloved hand up for Fiona to take as she got closer. Fiona reached for it. The grip was strong. Fiona figured that meant she had to grip back just as hard, like a handshake. People didn't respect anyone with a limp wrist. That was what she'd always heard. Charrling's bright blue eyes suddenly sparked with something dark, as if their strange lady version of a handshake was some sort of challenge to her.

"A strong grip you have, but my, what happened to your face? I apologize, that is a rude question. You have a birthmark, yes? You shouldn't worry too much about it. I'm sure Inferno will offer the best physicians to take care of that for you."

"Uh, no, it's not a birthmark," Fiona said. Was it a thing that royals were so blunt about everything? Fiona hoped that was what this was, but more and more, she was starting to sense a lot of resentment directed her way. Which was the exact thing she'd feared this whole time. "I had a reaction to a face cream earlier today, but Flare came to my rescue. She put some stuff on my face and now it's not as easy to notice."

"Well, I'm glad to hear it," said Charrling with a dazzling smile, the sort of thing that would almost make Fiona think she'd read the signals wrong before the woman opened her mouth again. "It must have looked dreadful before Flare was able to tend to it."

Okay, this woman was a bitch.

Fiona kept her breathing steady. If she inhaled a heavy

sigh, this woman was going to notice. She had a lot of practice dealing with bitching customers. She knew how to handle them when they were being pricks for no reason, and when they were angry and bitching over something small and stupid. She knew how to hold her cool and pretend as if there was nothing wrong with any of this.

"Flare did an amazing job. I'm glad to have made her as a friend."

The ice in Princess Charrling's eyes seemed to get just a little colder. "Indeed."

"It's very good to meet you."

The small voice caught Fiona off guard. She glanced to the side of the princess, and for the first time was able to give the other woman in the dining room her attention.

Princess Tinder glanced away quickly, her cheeks darkening with color. She was like a smaller, younger version of her mother. Only she wasn't giving off the hateful vibe. And a lot of pity swelled up inside Fiona's chest for the woman. Her mother might be a bitch, but Tinder wasn't a horrible person, as far as Fiona knew. She didn't deserve to have this happen to her.

Fiona didn't know if Tinder was even in love with Inferno, but she lived in the public eye. Being cast aside for another woman had to be an embarrassment, at the very least.

"It's very nice to meet you, your highness," Fiona said.

Tinder didn't look back at her; she just softly shook her head. "I'm not a princess."

She wasn't? Fuck. That's right, a king's sister was a princess, but his nieces didn't get that title. What did Fiona call someone who was related to royalty but not actually a royal?

"Oh, well, sometimes the papers call you a princess," Fiona said, trying to be helpful.

Tinder pressed her lips tightly together, her brows furrowing before she pushed herself to her feet with a small uttered apology and walked swiftly to the door.

Inferno appeared in the doorway just as Tinder made it to him. She barely stopped herself from bumping into his chest.

Inferno blinked down at her, a soft smile pulling at his lips. "You decided to come?"

Tinder's hands clenched into fists. Fiona couldn't see her face, but Tinder lowered her head. She fidgeted in place a moment before stepping past Inferno and leaving the dining room.

Inferno looked back at the direction his cousin, his expression troubled. He turned his gaze to the people in the dining room, as though wondering what had happened. When his gaze landed on Fiona, he seemed to forget all about Tinder, and he rushed towards her, holding his hands out and placing his palms on her nearly bare shoulders, a smile on his face.

"You're...you look beautiful. I'm glad you felt well enough to come."

She quickly forgot about the fact that he hadn't left her a choice in the matter when that rush of desire and warmth flooded into her. It almost felt as if someone had just turned a tap of hot water on full blast over her body with no intention of turning it off. He had a glow about him. The sight of him, even the sound of his voice, relieved her, took so much of the pressure off her shoulders that she'd felt.

She was glad he was here. She hadn't exactly been in any danger, but she felt safer. She felt blanketed in his strength. "Of course I'm here, where you needed me to be," she said softly. God, she needed to get a grip. She had to look away from his eyes. She was getting sucked into them.

Fiona became aware that Inferno was gently easing her behind him. He stared down at his aunt with a pleasant expression on his face, but his eyes were just as cold as Princess Charrling's had been a moment ago. "What happened?"

Charrling lifted her teacup to her lips. "My daughter is heartbroken. Of course she wouldn't wish to be here."

"Are we late?" Fiona looked back. Blaze and Ember had appeared and were standing next to their sister.

"Just in time," Flare murmured, not taking her gaze from Inferno, who was staring intently at Charrling. He growled, and his lips pulled back enough to show the whites of his teeth and long fangs that were growing larger.

Fiona's eyes widened when she realized his color was changing, but not because he was angry. There were also red scales forming around his jaw.

"Fiona is my mate now, do you understand that?" Inferno said through his teeth.

Oh God, his eyes were glowing now.

Flare attempted to intervene. "Inferno—"

He ignored his sister. "I asked if you understood that. You will answer me immediately."

Fiona's throat dried up. It was an event in and of itself to see Inferno this angry, this growly, this...*dangerous* looking. The way he seemed eager to protect her, even from a spiteful relative, was kind of a turn on. It was stupid, but it made her feel almost special to him.

The moment was interrupted when another set of double doors opened on the opposite side of the dining room, and several men walked in pushing metal trollies. They wore black suits with vests, white-collared shirts, and black ties, but the white aprons gave them away as the wait staff.

Blaze helped Fiona to her seat, and Ember guided Inferno to his, then the siblings took their places at the table. If the wait staff sensed any tension in the room, they ignored it as they swiftly surrounded the table and lifted lids off of their steaming dishes, revealing foods that Fiona would never have dreamed she'd see at a casual family dinner.

Charrling never so much as glanced up at her nephew. Fiona could tell that, even though Inferno was the one who was going to be king, she thought herself to be his superior. "I have no idea what you're talking about, nephew. Of course she is your mate if she is Istavan blood."

"She is," Inferno said with a snap of his teeth. "Do I have a reason to be concerned that she will have an allergic reaction to the food presented here?"

This time, Charrling's eyes flashed dangerously up at them. "I am certain I have no idea what you're talking about, and I would appreciate the change in tone."

Inferno growled at her. Fiona saw that in addition to more scales, Inferno had also started to sprout horns from his jawline and parts of his face.

Ember leaned over, placed his hand on his brother's shoulder, and whispered something into his ear. Whatever it was, it seemed to calm Inferno as he glanced down at Fiona. The scales, and even the few small horns retracted back into his skin.

Fiona hadn't even considered that what happened to her face might have been anything other than an allergy or skin sensitivity. But Inferno thought this woman had done that?

Holy shit. That was terrifying as all hell.

"I'll have questions for you later, Aunt," Inferno said in what was clearly a threat.

"I understand, though it would be best if we could clear this up after photographs."

"Pictures?"

The word came from her and Inferno's mouths at the same time. They briefly looked at each other before Inferno glared back at his aunt. "We will be taking no photographs today."

"But you must," Charrling announced, glancing up at her nephew as if he'd lost his mind. "Though I suppose it is a shame Tinder won't be here to give her support for your new mating, I am certain the public will not hold that against a happy couple."

Fiona wanted to laugh at that. "Lady, do you even use Facebook or Twitter?" People were going to rip them to shreds. Fiona's stomach sank. The public adored Tinder.

Oh no.

She sat through a whole presentation today to understand the intricacies of dragon mating. The general public wasn't going to understand what it meant that Inferno had found his natural mate. How the situation nullified his agreement with Tinder. They were going to look at it like a tragedy, and at Tinder like a victim. Inferno wouldn't be the focus of online hate. He was the future king of dragons, well-liked, and good-looking as all hell.

Fiona would be seen as the homewrecker. The villain in this story. Millions of people were going to start combing through her recipe videos, her blog, profiles, for anything and everything they could use to make their judgments about her.

The thought made her sick.

Fiona barely realized that Charrling was glaring at her.

Probably for the rude way she'd just spoken to her, but she could hardly bring herself to care at that moment, not when she was about to puke.

"The press will, of course, need to see who their future king is choosing to be their queen. This is a matter of convention, not something done to be spiteful, no matter what you might think."

"And, what? Inferno and I don't get any say in when this happens?"

"They should be arriving soon," Charrling said, glancing back to one of the waiters. "Well? I would like the filet of salmon, please."

Fiona couldn't take anymore. She yanked herself away from the table and ran to the nearest flower vase. She grabbed onto it and threw up what little she had in her stomach.

13

—————

Inferno watched his mate be ill in one of the flower vases, horrified that this could happen at all. He'd once puked in a decorative vase, but that had been when he was only twelve years old, his parents had still been alive, and he'd gotten food poisoning.

It had been just moments before when Inferno had walked into the dining room, taken one look at his beautiful mate, and felt like the world was set right. So much of the tension in his shoulders had vanished at her light, even with Tinder storming off.

Now he looked from Flare, moving quickly to help Fiona pull back her long hair so it wouldn't be tangled in the flowers, back to his aunt.

Charrling sipped at her tea between delicate bites of her salmon. She wrinkled her nose when Fiona groaned, though she said nothing of the noises in the room or the smell. She pushed her plate away with a sigh. "I am finished. One cannot expect to have an appetite after a scene like that."

"You caused that!"

Inferno's voice boomed in the dining room, echoing off the far walls, and Charrling finally looked at him, as if she was only now ready to take his anger seriously.

"Inferno?" Flare asked uncertainly.

Inferno hardly spared his sister a glance, though when he did, he noted the way Fiona was also looking at him. Her flaming red hair and that yellow dress gave her flesh a deathly pale look to it. He didn't like that. He didn't like knowing that his mate had been so hurt, and right in front of him, too, by someone in his own family.

Inferno growled, reminding himself that this woman sitting before him was his aunt, the woman who used to spoil him as a child, who was the sister of his dead father, and whom he loved.

Though her behavior was severely testing that love at the moment.

Inferno turned to his brothers. "The both of you, go and stall the reporters. I am not here, and neither is Fiona. There will be no pictures, and there will be no story." Ember could be diplomatic, and Blaze was hot-headed and scrappy enough to get what he wanted in most cases.

"Got it," Blaze said, spinning on his heel and running out of the room before anything else needed to be said.

Ember simply nodded, his gaze flicking down to their aunt before he met and held Inferno's eyes. They didn't say anything, didn't have to. Ember turned and walked out, slower and more deliberate than the way Blaze had.

Blaze might attempt to fuck with the press. Unless he happened to think any of their women were good to look at. Ember would balance out that act and see to it they left the property, and that none of them tried to sneak back on.

"Can I assume that the photographers who attempted to sneak onto the grounds were brought here by you as well?"

Charrling glared at him. "No. You cannot. Joseph," she signaled to her guard, "you may escort me back to my rooms now, please."

"We have more to discuss, Charrling," Inferno said as she walked by.

His aunt tensed at the door, her anger clear and wafting from her, but she said nothing to him. She continued on her way out.

What was happening to his home? When did he lose so much control? Had he ever had control at all? Perhaps he was only now seeing the pests burrowing in the foundation.

"I'm sorry." Fiona was a few feet away from him, her head turned down, a hand over her mouth, as pale as he'd ever seen someone.

Yet she was still lovely, still his, and now Inferno knew that he didn't have to only protect her from whatever forces had been at work to harm her in her apartment. He was going to have to protect her from the other royals in this house who did not want her here. He would have to protect her from the jealous nobles, and the harsh words of the press and society at large.

Inferno walked over to his mate, nodding to his sister. "Thank you for tending to her."

Flare, usually a little too upbeat and energetic for her own good, at that moment seemed a little more subdued and cautious.

"Yeah, don't worry about it," she said, turning her attention back to Fiona. "I think all the events from today have added up. Fiona should get some rest and take some time to let everything sink in."

Fiona barely let herself glance up at Inferno. He briefly glanced up to the vase that had been soiled, noting a few of the maids standing at the servant's doors, waiting to swoop in and take the offending item away. He nodded to them to enter. They did, and they moved quickly. This did not seem to please Fiona, who grew paler as she watched one of the maids lift the vase and take it out of the room while another sprayed the surface it had been sitting on and wiped it down. It was as though knowing others would be cleaning up after her caused her more humiliation than it helped. Inferno couldn't understand why that was.

"They will take it away, and you should think nothing of it. I will settle things with my aunt and my cousin."

That didn't seem to make her feel better. She hid her face in her hands now, as if his words made the problem worse.

"I'll take her back to her room," Flare offered. "Come on, Fiona."

"No." Inferno reached out, unthinkingly swooping his arm around Fiona's waist before his little sister could make off with her. Eric and Fiona's guards, as well as his own, quickly gathered, ready to follow them. "She's staying with me tonight, in my apartments. It will be safest there." He didn't add that it would also give him the most peace of mind.

She was going to Inferno's rooms.

And the main thing that was on her mind was that she hoped he would let her use some mouthwash in his bathroom right away. She kept her face diverted away from him the whole walk, hoping to avoid disgusting him.

Inferno had been angry with his aunt, and she knew he wasn't mad at her, but some of that anger was still with him as he took large and fast strides down the halls, and she hurried to keep up with him. She was kind of glad for the speed. She didn't want to risk that one of the reporters Blaze and Ember had gone after would get around.

"Can I use your bathroom?"

"You don't need to ask," Inferno said, pointing. "It's down there, the door to the left in my office. It connects to my bedroom."

Fiona ignored the heat in her face, walking across the apartment. They entered in an extended living room, complete with bookcases lining most of one wall, a flat screen television bolted above the fireplace, and a couple of couches facing each other across from a coffee table, with some reading chairs in the back corner.

It was larger than her apartment back home.

She passed by the office he indicated, and took a moment to observe the regal and professional atmosphere of it; more bookcases along the walls, made of dark mahogany, and packed with thick hardcovers of what looked like law books or encyclopedias, hefty tomes that important politicians would need for reference while ruling their people and negotiating with other world leaders.

She let herself into Inferno's private bathroom, which lit up when she entered. She sucked in a breath, not ready for the luxurious spa-like accommodations.

Everything was gleaming marble, and clean. The bathroom smelled vaguely of his aftershave, the only personal scent she'd been able to pick up since walking into his rooms. The sitting area and his office both held aromas of wood and leather, but in here she could smell Inferno, intense with a hint of musk.

His countertop had two sinks in it, and she realized that this apartment wasn't designed for a bachelor. They were made for the royal couple. Was this the heir's apartment, or the kings? It was undoubtedly ornate enough to be either. In any case, there was no hint of anything of Tinder's in there. Had she not lived here with him, or had they cleaned out her things that quickly? A wave of jealousy, and embarrassment, rushed over her at the thought.

It didn't matter. She was going to be his wife soon. She had feelings for him, and she knew he felt something for her too. She just had to be brave enough to face him and to follow the feelings down the road enough to see where it went. At the very least, if things didn't work out, he had promised that he would give her a bakery, so it wouldn't all be a loss.

But she couldn't help but wonder what it would be like if it did work out. What if they did find love, and have children? What if she did become queen?

The feeling of rising panic had her shaking the thoughts away, and looking around the bathroom for what she needed. In a way, she'd almost expected an attendant to be in the bathroom, ready to offer her what she needed, but they'd been alone since entering the apartments. It was actually kind of nice.

She grabbed the mouthwash first, opening the cap and taking a full mouthful of what was inside. She swigged it around thoroughly, eager to get the horrible taste out of her mouth and to forget about what had happened in the first place.

God, she was so embarrassed.

She spit, and then just because she didn't feel like she was done, she reached for the toothpaste tube.

She brushed as well as she could with her finger before rinsing her mouth out under the tap, then she took stock of herself in the mirror.

Her lipstick was gone, making her look even paler than

she felt, but luckily all the stuff Flare had put onto her face to hide the burning seemed to be holding up, along with her mascara. Though, she supposed she had bigger things to worry about if someone from inside the palace had tried to hurt her.

Fiona inhaled a deep breath, let it out, then did it again. She was going to be all right. She was going to be all right.

She'd never known Charrling could be such a bitch in real life.

"Stupid reporters," she muttered.

The mirror beeped at her, text appearing over the glass, and a woman's voice called out to her through it. *"Would you like to prepare an interview?"*

Fiona jumped back with a gasp. She nearly slipped with her heels still on but managed to catch herself.

The text was still on the mirror, letting her know precisely where the voice had come from. "Uh, no thank you," she said.

"Confirmed."

There was a sudden knock outside the bathroom door. "You all right in there?"

Fiona looked to the door, then to the mirror, and back again before she moved towards the door, opening it. Inferno stood there, tall and imposing.

Fiona pointed back behind her. "Your mirror is alive."

Inferno glanced to the mirror, and then back at her with a soft smile. "No, don't worry about that. She's just programmed to respond to certain keywords."

"She?"

"The Queen. I thought it was a funny joke when I had her installed."

Fiona wasn't sure if she should smile along with him or

not. It seemed more or less like this was kind of a creepy robot thing in the bathroom.

"You might want to warn your guests before 'The Queen' scares them half to death," she said.

Inferno laughed. "Don't worry, she's not all that smart, and she's not secretly watching us, or planning how she's going to kill us."

"Good to hear."

"Queen, turn on my favorite radio station, please."

Something started to play at his request. It took Fiona a couple of seconds before she recognized the Guns N Roses song.

"You're a classic rock kind of guy?"

"Seventies and some eighties," Inferno said, smiling down at her before turning back to the mirror. "Queen, give me the weather, please."

The mirror changed, revealing a sunny landscape with some blue clouds, birds chirping as they flew by, and the temperature in large numbers.

"She also has access to the palace camera system. Queen, show me the front yard."

The mirror changed and revealed the front yard, just as he commanded. There was a small crowd out there, and what looked to be an awful lot of people with cameras. Fiona squinted, then realized Blaze and Ember were down there, giving interviews.

"Can we hear what they're saying?"

"If we want to. Do you want to?"

Fiona watched the men and women in the mirror, and the way Blaze and Ember seemed to handle them, answering intense questions with pleasant smiles.

"I don't think I want to know what they're asking about me."

Inferno nodded. "Fair enough. Mirror mode."

The mirror turned back into a regular mirror.

"I'll give you a tablet that will be able to see everything the mirror will show you. We have a whole system that was designed with top-level security. There's no camera in it, so nothing can get hacked to watch you or me do anything, but we'll be able to see what's going on outside, and before you ask, I don't keep cameras in the guest rooms, or anyone's bathroom."

Fiona hadn't even thought about that, but now that he mentioned it, she was glad he'd brought it up. "Thanks for clarifying."

Inferno touched her cheek. Fiona wasn't sure what it was, but the touch shocked her back into that state of want and arousal that she hadn't felt since throwing up.

"Why am I feeling this again?"

"Feeling what?"

Fiona briefly pressed her lips together. "Like I'm about to go out of my damned mind when you touch me. It wasn't like this a second ago. I nearly forgot about the heat thing."

Inferno smiled down at her. "Do you really think that if one mate were feeling sick, the other would still have an instinct to copulate?"

"I guess not," she said, still feeling out of control about the entire thing. "It's still weird, though."

"It is, and I'm sorry for the way Charrling treated you."

Fiona shrugged, attempting to go for not looking like she cared so much about what that woman thought of her. "She's pissed off at me because I'm stealing her daughter's fiancée. I think I'd be pissed off, too."

"The only people I need to be gentle with in all of this is you and Tinder. Charrling has no right to be upset or to lash out at you. Tinder is the only one who can be upset, but I would certainly never allow her to lash out at you. Fortunately, that's not her way."

Fiona could believe that. The other woman had left the room rather than stick around with her. "Thank you."

Inferno cocked his head to the side a little. "For what?"

She looked up at him and then had to look away again quickly. "For being...I don't know, really good about all of this."

Inferno nodded, though he glanced away as if he didn't entirely agree with her assessment of the situation. "I'll keep you hidden away, for now. The time will eventually come when you will have to face those men outside, but when that happens, I promise you, it will be on our terms."

"O-okay," Fiona said, suddenly finding it hard to gather her words.

The heat in Inferno's voice put his namesake to shame.

He nodded, but then something in his face changed. He went from smoldering to something darker, and without another word, he turned and walked out, leaving her alone, as if he was fleeing from something. A man like Inferno fleeing from anything seemed all kinds of wrong, but Fiona was too shocked to do anything except stand there, wondering what the hell happened.

14

Inferno needed to put some distance between himself and his mate. He felt awful for it, but despite his earlier words about the instinct to mate being gone, that hadn't entirely been true. Instinct was instinct after all, and while the scent of sickness was enough to dull the urge, it was still there.

Fiona would feel that numbing of her instincts more than Inferno simply because she was the one who had been ill, but that didn't change the fact that he still wanted her.

Badly.

Right. Well, she was here in his rooms, they were alone, and the moment she felt better, the chances were good that she would be coming to him.

He might not need to do anything at all.

That was a shame. There was always something fun about the chase, though at the same time, Inferno was eager to see his mate when she was in the throes of passion, and throwing herself at his feet. He was a greedy man, but while Fiona stayed in the bathroom, he figured he might as well do a little work.

He stepped out the main door to his apartments and motioned to Eric. The guards were standing at attention on the opposite wall, hands held in front of them, sunglasses on, but Inferno could still tell they were alert, along with the other men on duty.

"Have you heard anything from Ember's men on that pot of green goo that was put on her face?"

"Nothing much yet," Eric said. "We sent the whole cart of beauty compounds for testing, and the lab knows to give me a call. If we find out anything, where it came from, how poisonous it was, and if it will cause any lasting damage, I'll get the information to you right away."

Inferno nodded. "Good."

"Yes, however, if you are unavailable," Eric's head moved to the direction of the door, where Fiona waited for Inferno, "I will go to Ember or Blaze, whichever one of them is immediately available."

Inferno couldn't help the light smirk that tugged at the corner of his mouth. Right, Eric knew what a newly mated couple had on their mind.

The smirk melted away quickly. Inferno had to get serious. "I don't want the press getting wind of the fact that Fiona seems to be in danger. If there is any question of why we have increased security, I want them to assume the added personnel in the palace is because of Fiona's recent arrival, and because of the reporters that tried to gain access to the grounds this afternoon."

"Yes, sir."

Inferno thought quickly. Even though Fiona was in his chambers right now, he didn't cherish the thought of leaving her alone for too long. "Put a watch on Charrling and Tinder, and not the usual guards. Get someone in there who is usually on my staff. We likely won't be able to catch her causing trouble, but an extra set of eyes and ears is always useful."

"I'll see to it that it's done," Eric promised.

What else could Inferno do? He was a dragon shifter, a prince, and an alpha. He wasn't used to this feeling of helplessness. It was unnerving, to say the least. Having a mate, a human, something so utterly fragile, was going to be the death of him; he could tell already. But even fragile humans could build up their strengths. Fiona likely would not be getting into a battle with anyone in her life, but if he could prepare her for the chance that it might happen, he would be able to breathe easier.

"Tomorrow Fiona is to start training in self-defense techniques. The shooting range, gym, and trainers should be ready for her."

Eric nodded, hardly missing a beat. "Yes, sire, they're on call. Just say the word whenever you want to go down there."

Inferno nodded. "Another thing, make sure to set up a selection of sidearms and holsters appropriate for human female-sized hands. We're not just going down there to play around. She's going to keep the piece on her and needs to be able to wield it effectively when the time comes."

Eric nodded, blanching just a little. It was dangerous to have a novice walking around with a gun, but if Inferno had decided that it was more dangerous for Fiona to be unarmed, the guards would just have to be on extra alert. "I'll get on that right away."

"See to it that you do." Inferno needed to get back into his chambers and to his mate. He already felt as if he'd been out here long enough. He shut the door behind him, barely stopping himself from slamming it.

Inferno clenched and unclenched his fists. He was irritated now. All that talk of threats had made him agitated.

Red scales appeared spottily over his arms, hardening into their protective forms that would create a barrier around him that was almost akin to steel armor.

He needed to calm himself. Fiona was here. She was alive and well, and just because everything was going to shit and he had no one's face to launch his fist into did not mean he would not eventually get his revenge. He would have it soon enough, and his mate would be able to live in this palace, her birthright, in safety, just as she was meant to.

"Fiona?"

She called back to him right away, which was good; it allowed him to relax. "I'm right here," she called.

Still in the bathroom, though the door was open. He saw her staring at the mirror with a transfixed expression on her face. Inferno frowned, stepping beside her. "What is it?" He looked up at the mirror, noted what his mate was looking at, and his eyes popped wide open. "Oh."

Fiona lifted a hand, pointing. "Isn't that your aunt?"

"It is," Inferno said, his emotions flicking through scandalized, furious, and then acceptance at the heated activity going on between Charrling and her head bodyguard, Joseph.

Inferno couldn't look away. He certainly had known that Joseph had been loyal to Charrling, but he had to wonder how they had both managed to keep this under the radar for so long.

They weren't fucking, Inferno could tell, and it wasn't because they were both still fully clothed.

There were ways around that, after all.

"I just...I just wanted to see what she was doing. I was mad. I didn't think I'd catch her doing...*this*." Fiona still sounded very much in a daze as she stared at the screen.

"Are they allowed to be doing that? I mean, they're not going to get into trouble or anything, are they?"

Inferno shook his head. He couldn't help but smile at the question while he pushed the manual button that would set the glass back to mirror mode and remove the scene from their eyes. "She is an adult, and she can do whatever she wants. If anything, I'm rather pleased you would care whether or not she'd get in trouble for this, considering what happened between you two earlier." It said a lot about the character of his mate, and he was happy with that. He was glad to know she was the sort of woman who would be worried for someone who had treated her ill.

It was the makings of a good queen.

Inferno was more curious about Charrling's situation. How long had this been going on? How serious was it? Sure, Joseph was below her station, and she could be holding out for a better offer, but at her age, she shouldn't be worrying about that kind of thing. She could marry Joseph and have a real life with him at her side, not just guarding her back.

Fiona looked at the second bathroom entrance, the one that led to his bedroom. "What now?"

"I hardly think that what we just saw set the mood," Inferno said, half laughing. The sound of Fiona's giggle warmed his whole body. "I think maybe we should have a sort of check-in, see how you're doing. Are you feeling better?"

She nodded. "It's quiet in here, which makes it a little easier to calm down. And it's nice too, nicer than most kidnapped people probably get."

Inferno looked down at her, raising a single brow.

"What? It's pretty fucked up."

"Do you feel like a prisoner?"

Fiona pressed her lips together, briefly looking away

from him, though her eyes went back to the mirror, and he supposed she was looking at the both of them standing there together instead of imagining what had just been on the screen. "No, but how do you think I feel? I'm not exactly a welcomed guest. I have none of my stuff from home. I'm supposed to be getting married to a stranger..."

The lack of certainty didn't sound so pleasing.

Even less pleasing than that was this new clench he felt in his gut, the idea that bringing his mate here, and claiming her as his own, was possibly the worst thing he could have done for her.

The side of her face that was still red was proof enough that she wasn't ready for this sort of life. A woman who aspired to be a baker and own her own shop may not be what the world was looking for in royalty, but what mattered the most was what Fiona was looking for, wasn't it?

"I'll make you a deal."

She looked at him.

Inferno rubbed his jaw. "Stay with me for a little while longer. This isn't an order. It's a request. You can decline, and I'll send you home right now, with guards. That part isn't up for negotiation."

The tension in Fiona's shoulders was immediate, and it did nothing to ease the clenching in Inferno's gut. He rarely got a feeling like that, and only when something bad was about to happen.

"Is that even possible? To just let your mate go?"

"Only when the situation is dire."

Fiona finally looked at him, and not through the mirror this time. "Is it dire?"

Inferno wet his lips. He felt young again, vulnerable and aching for this woman to want him.

"I don't know. I don't want to risk it either. I know you're not comfortable here. I also know that someone did that to your skin."

The thought that someone had did this intentionally danced around in her head, but she wouldn't let it sink it. It was almost too much to deal with. "I was told it would heal up just fine."

And it would because Inferno was going to get the best doctors and dermatologists to make sure she never so much as noticed a difference whenever she looked into a mirror.

"It will," Inferno nodded. "But, if I've asked too much of you, then you should be able to go back to the life you can thrive in."

She didn't stop frowning at him. He could have been speaking another language for all it mattered. "What about you? I thought...I mean, I guess you could have children with someone else, but won't your real heirs come from...well, me?"

She was right, but he couldn't tell her. He wouldn't tell her that, after seeing her, after knowing she existed, if she decided to leave, he wouldn't replace her. He would give the throne to Blaze and be done with it. Inferno wouldn't be without his mate. He couldn't. A dragon who lost his mate would live the rest of his days heartbroken and in mourning. He wouldn't be fit to rule, and he'd never make a lasting relationship with someone else.

He wouldn't tell her this, though. He didn't want her to make a decision based on what would happen to him. He wanted her to choose what was right for her.

"All you need to know is that if you want out, I'll still give you the bakery. You can have it in your name, or we'll set you up somewhere under a new name, for your protection. I'll see to it you're cared for. And my people will still work to figure out who was responsible for the attack on you last night."

She crossed her arms over her chest and narrowed her eyes at him. "You said you wanted to make me a deal. One of my options is to go home; tell me what the other is." She sounded irritated now, something he'd hoped wouldn't happen but wasn't shocked to hear.

"You're angry."

"It just doesn't sound like something my true love would be doing. Throwing me away when things get hard."

"Giving you the business of your dreams is hardly throwing you away like trash."

Her brows came together. Fiona pressed her lips together, as if she wanted to say something to him, maybe to shout at him, but didn't. Was she choosing not to because she was fearful of what she would say? Inferno was suddenly very eager to know what it was she wanted to shout at him.

He had to leave. The heat between them, even as they were having this almost fight, was too much. The scorching gaze of her eyes, the anger, the disappointment, and her combined beauty was enough to make him want to grab her, to yank her towards him and crush his mouth over hers, proving to her that he had no intention of letting her go no matter the cost.

He shook the thought from his mind. No. Not *no matter the cost*. The cost could be her life, and it was a stupid, idiotic risk to take.

Best to walk away. He would come for her later.

"H-hey! Where are you going?"

Inferno didn't answer her. He marched to the front apartment door, knowing she was following him, but he shut the door quickly before she could leave his rooms with him.

He counted on her not to follow him. He couldn't have her chasing him around the palace. He stopped, looking back at the guards, and nodded to Eric. "Make sure she stays put."

When Fiona didn't emerge from the apartment, Inferno sucked back a heavy breath. He turned and continued walking away.

15
___

Fiona didn't sleep that night.

Not very well, at least.

Mostly, she lay in the overly large bed that would have taken up the entire space in the living room of her apartment. She was surprised it didn't have a canopy.

Fiona put herself in the exact middle of it because then it somehow seemed like slightly less of a waste of space, but she was lonely. She was trapped on her own tiny, private island, and while the sheets were soft, thick, and managed to keep her warm without overheating her like her quilt at home could do, she was lonely as all hell.

And angry. And sad.

Inferno had gone through all of that, had kidnapped her from her home—he'd saved her life, too, but currently, that wasn't the point—and after insisting to her that she was the long-lost princess in a line of humans who could truly mate with dragons...

She didn't even know why this was bothering her. She hadn't wanted to be here in the first place. She had only become interested in the deal when Inferno had offered her a bakery.

Now he was talking about getting rid of her.

Fiona's fingers clenched the sheets. She couldn't stop gripping them, worrying them. She was going to tear a hole into the quilt any moment now. Maybe it was because she was imagining it was Inferno's neck she was holding onto so tightly.

He wanted to send her back, something that honestly should have thrilled her. If he was serious about taking care of her, about giving her the business of her dreams and her freedom, then it was akin to winning the lottery.

There was a time when she would have jumped at the chance to let some rich guy take care of all her bills while she flitted off to follow her dreams. No commitment, no sex, no bearing children, no relationship, and everything would be taken care of. Who didn't want that?

This was somehow different. This was something Fiona wasn't comfortable with, and the fact that she was alone in this enormous bed, in a room that was bigger than her apartment, which was part of a series of rooms that was larger than most houses...

It was just lonely. That was the only word she had to describe it. Inferno was supposed to be here with her. He'd said he was going to take her, and now that he wasn't here, it left her body wanting. The fact that the sheets smelled like him didn't help.

Fiona had been under the impression that the staff around here would have been cleaning the sheets and replacing them every single night, but it seemed that wasn't the case, because all Fiona could smell was Inferno.

It was making her all kinds of crazy.

At some point, Fiona did nod off. She knew this because,

when she snapped her eyes open again, even though it was still dark, she felt as if she'd been sleeping. But she also felt as if someone had just been in the room with her.

Her heart pounded, eager anticipation pushing through her as she sat up, and Inferno stood off on the far side of the room.

Was he here for her? Had he changed his mind about letting her leave?

More importantly, was he going to come into bed with her? "Inferno?"

He stepped back. She couldn't see the expression on his face, but it was clear she'd embarrassed him by catching him there.

She wasn't embarrassed in the least. "You can come over here. I'm not mad at you." *Please come over here.* She wanted him to go to her so badly she could taste it. Her body felt tight, her nipples perked, and absolutely everything inside her called out to him.

So when he turned away from her, walking out, Fiona sat there frozen.

And embarrassed.

She listened to the dull thudding of his footsteps as he walked out. A door opened somewhere, not the front door to the bedroom. Had there been another entrance?

Either way, he took it, because Fiona listened hard and did not hear him come back.

Without knowing why, and without her body so much as giving her a warning, Fiona burst into tears. She fell back against her pillow, hating him so much. Hating him for bringing her here. Hating him for teasing her, for making her want him and then being aloof and distant when her body ached to have him.

The stupid mating. Fiona punched her pillow several

times. She imagined it was Inferno's stupid face to make herself feel better.

And then she imagined his face when she had to touch herself, to make the physical ache she felt from him bearable.

Fiona woke up to natural sunlight. She groaned, listening to the sharp hiss of metal on metal as the curtains were pulled open.

She sat up suddenly, startled that someone was in the room with her.

No one was there. The curtains were opening on their own. They must have been on a timer.

Fiona rolled her eyes and flopped back down onto the bed, pulling her pillow over her face to block out the light.

Hideous sunlight. She wanted it off her body.

It didn't seem as if she was going to get what she wanted when she heard a door in the apartment open and then shut again. Then she heard talking. There was more than one person out there. One of them sounded like Inferno, but she so didn't care. Fiona groaned, pressing more pillows to her head to try to drown out the noise.

Which was about the time when Inferno walked into her room. Or rather, his room.

"Get up. I let you sleep in by two hours."

Fiona didn't get up, and she didn't lift her face out of the mountains of comfortable pillows. She did, however, raise her middle finger to him.

Someone snorted a laugh, but it was cut short.

"Fiona," Inferno said in what he probably thought was a playful growl. He didn't say anything else as he grabbed the comforter off Fiona's body and yanked it away. Her bubble of perfect body temperature went away with it, the chill in the room that assaulted her so suddenly made her curl up in reflex.

And lift her head enough to yell at the idiot. "What are you doing? For all you know, I was naked under here!"

Inferno smiled as if he'd been hoping to see that exact thing, never mind the fact that she could see Eric and a few other guards through the doorway, politely pretending to look at anything else.

"You're perfectly decent; now get up." Inferno tossed the comforter on the floor in the corner, where Fiona wouldn't be able to snatch it back without getting out of bed. She was glad that she'd decided to ransack his room to find a t-shirt and boxer shorts to sleep in.

She grumbled, forcing herself away from the bed. God, this was such a nice bed. If Inferno was interested in kicking her out of the palace for her safety, she hoped he would let her take this mattress with her.

Inferno sniffed at the air, a slight frown pulling at his brows.

Fiona glared at him. "What's with you?" She was still irritable at having to get up out of bed. The clock on the nightstand said it wasn't even seven in the morning yet.

And Inferno said he'd let her sleep in by two hours? Jesus Christ.

"Eric, close the door, right now."

Fiona froze. She didn't know what the hell that was supposed to be about, but the sudden and sharp tone in Inferno's voice had her stopping as if she'd just done something wrong.

Eric didn't ask questions. He didn't even look as if what Inferno had just ordered was out of the ordinary. The door quickly closed, with a very quiet click.

"Hey, wait, what's going on?" Fiona wasn't sure she wanted to be rid of witnesses. She was afraid of Inferno's angry expression and the way his nostrils flared when he faced her.

"Okay, I'll get dressed. What the hell is your—hey!"

Fiona didn't have the chance to ward off his attack. He came at her suddenly, his hands, strong and demanding, wrapping his arms around the waist and pulling her up to her knees on the bed, her sleepy body pressed against him.

Her body didn't stay sleepy for long. An eruption went up inside of her, sparking every nerve with heat and excitement. Not a thought went through her mind as her lips moved to connect with his.

His mouth against her was hot. Hotter than his namesake, and the sudden rush of it all was almost too much for her to bear. Fiona moaned. Her mind felt dizzy, her body melted against the kiss, and his body, as if she was in a sauna, and her muscles were forced to relax against him.

He pulled his mouth away from hers with a hard gasp, as if it was a struggle to keep away from her, to not kiss her.

"You touched yourself last night."

Fiona blinked, her brain needing a minute to catch up with what she'd just heard. "What?"

Inferno's eyes positively burned. She could see a fire crackling within them as if his inner dragon was breathing fire as he pushed her towards the bed. "I can smell you in the room."

Fiona found herself pulling him down on the mattress on top of her.

"What did you think I was going to do after you left?" She asked between kisses. "A whole day telling me we were mates. A whole day of this spark between us. You whisking me off to your room, and then leaving me here alone." She licked his ear, and then for good measure nipped it.

Inferno growled a noise that didn't belong to a dragon, but to a man who had a great need to be with his mate. As he rocked his body against hers, they moved to the center of the bed, and then he pinned her arms on either side of her while he trailed kisses down her neck. She felt so good but also felt such torture. She needed him to touch her, everywhere. She needed to touch him.

She freed her arms and reached for his hair, which had been tied back and was now becoming undone. She pushed her fingers into the dark strands and gripped hard, making a mess of how neat it had been. He looked at her, breathless, and she used her grip to pull him back to her mouth.

She also wanted to show him that she was part of this, too. She was not just going to lie here and let him do whatever he wanted to her. She was going to participate. She was going to make him just as crazy as he'd been making her.

As if to prove it, Fiona pushed one of his shoulders, guiding him off her of her and down on the bed on his back. She went on top of him, feeling the intensity of the heat of his pelvis against hers, through the thin clothes she was wearing, and the slacks he had on. Fiona couldn't help the small moan that escaped her.

The forward thrust of his hips against hers, the substantial length of his cock she felt beneath his pants, it all created a buzz inside her head and body that she could hardly ignore. The pleasure was instant as if she was just as frustrated and desperate as the night before.

This was what she wanted. This was everything she needed.

At least he wasn't going to walk away from her this time.

He'd better not.

To make sure, Fiona stilled, putting her hands on his

chest and leaning down until her lips tickled his ear. "Don't you dare walk away this time," she purred.

She felt a shudder go through his body, and Inferno shook his head.

"I mean it," she pulled her head up, to meet his eyes, smiling as she did. "I'll kill you if you do."

Inferno smiled at her, his eyes dancing in amusement at the threat. Typically, it was not a good idea in any way, shape, or form to threaten a member of the royal family, but he was currently between her legs, grinding against her, so she was sure she could get away with it.

Instead of saying anything in response, Inferno pushed his strong hand beneath her tiny tank top and found her breast. He massaged it, his fingers playing against her hardened nipples. Fiona closed her eyes against the sudden pleasure of it, arching her back.

Her body wanted more. Not even in just the obvious sense, not only because it felt good. Fiona could have been dying of thirst at that moment, and given the choice of walking to Inferno, or walking to a glass of water, she would have chosen Inferno.

His heated mouth pressed softly against her neck. She could smell his aftershave. It surrounded her, made her moan and push her body harder against his, her chest more firmly against his hand.

Inferno lifted her tank top abruptly and replaced his palm with his mouth. Fiona's eyes flew open, her mouth dropping in a silent gasp. The heat, the wet heat of him, it was enough to make the muscles in her stomach and legs clench up. She felt his erection through his pants, and the vibration of his moan against her breast caused her brain fizzle out for a moment.

The longest, best moment of her life.

Fiona squirmed on top of him. This time she wouldn't let him get away. She wouldn't allow any interruption stop them from doing what felt so right. She needed to get their clothes off.

She crawled off of him, avoiding his grasp when he reached for her. A look of confusion crossed his face. She gave the dragon royal a warning look and pointed a finger at him. "Don't even think about moving," she said, her voice breathy as she shoved down the elastic waist of the shorts she'd borrowed, followed by her underwear.

Inferno grinned. "I think I'd like to know what you would do to me if I did walk away."

The next mission for her hands was to grab onto his belt, to fiddle with it until she finally loosened it enough that she could get his pants down.

"Don't think you want to know."

"But I do," Inferno said, offering her almost no help at all as she got his pants down. As if he was enjoying the way she was undressing him.

She looked up at him, shaking her head. "Honestly, at this point, I think if you tried to leave, I'd chase you out into the hallway while naked, and make quite a show of tackling you in front of all of your guards."

Inferno reacted in the last way she'd thought he would. He laughed. "I can run pretty fast. You might not catch me until the dining room."

His pants finally off, as well as his socks and shoes, she made her way up to his shirt, pushing it up and feeling every ab muscle in his ripped chest as she did so. This time, he helped her by getting the shirt off his head and arms. "At least now we'd both be naked, running in front of people."

"Almost naked." They both looked down to the boxer

shorts that he was still wearing. Her face reddened, a slight shyness finally creeping up in her.

Inferno, however, didn't seem about to let her determination disappear. He sat up, sliding his hand into Fiona's hair. He pulled her close and pressed his mouth to her lips once more. He chuckled even as he kissed her. It didn't entirely do away with her embarrassment, but it was a good start, and Fiona found herself able to relax again.

Fiona let herself get lost to the heat of it. It was easy. She didn't have to think about it too much. She just let herself get swept away.

This time, she let him lay her down underneath him and waited while he got rid of the last piece of cloth on his body. Then the heat of his mouth was back on hers, wonderful, but softer and less furious than they had been a moment ago. The slide of his tongue made her entire body buzz and tingle. Her sex swelled and filled with warmth as Inferno's hands moved all over her body, leaving a trail of invisible fire on every inch of her skin.

"Are you ready for this?" He asked, looking down at her with a tenderness she hadn't yet seen from him.

"Yes," she breathed, arching her body and reaching for him.

He caught her hand in his and kissed her palm. "You're the most beautiful woman I've ever seen. You know that?"

"I'd tell you how magnificent you are, but I'm sure you already know that." She responded.

His smile lit up her heart, and her body welcomed him on top of her. Her knees on both sides of his hips, she felt his smooth member press against her entrance, and he kissed her slowly while pushing, with just a little pressure at a time. When she wasn't sure how much more she could take, he stilled.

Her breath caught, body tensing as she adjusted to being taken.

Inferno exhaled a hard groan, and braced himself on his elbows, hovering over her, wincing, as if it were a challenge to be so still.

"I'm yours now, right?" Fiona asked.

"As much as I'm yours," he replied, kissing her hair and giving them a moment to breathe.

When Fiona felt used to the slight pain of him inside of her, she began to move her hips. The small encouragement had Inferno moving again, slowly at first, until they started to build a faster momentum.

Inferno's hips pushed forward and back. Fiona laced her fingers together at the back of his neck, locking him in place, keeping him close, so he had to look into her eyes. She needed to look into them, to see the affection there. They had a connection, something that he claimed was their natural mating instinct, and right then, she felt exactly how true it was, how they belonged together. How she would never feel for another man the way she felt for this majestic dragon prince.

A rumbling, growling noise escaped from deep within Inferno's chest. The push and pull of his hips increased. The strength at which he thrust forward made Fiona cry out.

More heat. More intensity. Every inch of her building toward a climax bigger than any one she'd had on her own. She was going to pop, but she wanted to hold off until he was there too.

"Are you close?" She asked, breathless, gripping his shoulders tight, knowing her nails would probably leave marks, but not caring because he seemed to like it.

She didn't hear him respond, because he started to pump harder, bracing one hand against his headboard as he slammed into her. It was more than enough to send her over the edge. Fiona's mouth found his, and she moaned as they connected. She couldn't hold back, and she didn't bother to try as her pleasure cascaded over her, taking control of her, making her body clench and unclench around Inferno, trapping him to her.

She pushed her hands into his hair and gripped him hard just because she could. His breath hitched, and he groaned. His body tensed until his already impressive body felt as solid as a rock in her arms. Their eyes locked, and he heaved a few, slow, and final thrusts into her before his body relaxed and he lowered himself on top of her, burying his face into her neck.

His body was heavy, but in a good way. She wanted this intimacy, to feel cocooned by him. The intense desire, the need to touch and be touched by him, to have him make love to her, was still there, but it was calmed. She was momentarily satiated.

Fiona smiled. She found Inferno's hand, and she laced her fingers with his. She had no idea what he was feeling, but she was glad he was here, and things seemed more like they could be worked out now instead of being pushed to the side.

"Wishing we could have done this last night when you came to see me, but I'm still happy for this."

"Hmm?" Inferno pushed himself off her chest.

It made it easier for her to breathe, but already she missed the warmth. Her whole body tingled with happiness, feeling the echo of him still on her. "Last night, when you came back. I don't know why you ran away so fast when I called out to you."

Inferno blinked at her, then frowned. "Are you sure you weren't just dreaming?"

Fiona wanted to laugh, but the look on his face made it clear he wasn't joking around. "No, I never have dreams that clear. You were right there," she motioned to the wall, but the smile slid from her face when he pushed himself off her body and left the bed.

The anger, no, the rage on his face told Fiona this was not a laughing matter.

Fiona followed his lead, putting her clothes back on. "Inferno, what's wrong? What's going on?"

He spared her a glance before yanking open the bedroom door. "I never came back to this room last night."

16

———

Fiona's head was spinning. Inferno charged through the hall and found the guards, shouting at them. She wasn't sure if she should follow, but then Leanne appeared, holding a stack of clothes and a basket of sealed beauty supplies. "M'lady, Prince Inferno sent me back to see to you. He's asked me to see that you have a shower and get ready for the day."

"Thank you, Leanne." She knew better than to ask the maid what was going on. The woman looked just as confused as she felt.

Leanne showed her how the shower worked and left behind the clothes and makeup, as well as instructions that she'd be in the bedroom if Fiona needed anything. Fiona was glad to have clean clothes and to be allowed to dress herself, but she did it all in a rush. Inferno was still shouting and she worried that Eric was in trouble. The redness on her face had gone down a bit, but she made sure to cover it up as much as she could. Best not give Inferno a reminder of anything else he was still angry about. She pulled on the clothes, and remembered the promise of self-defense lessons that Inferno had made. If these workout clothes were any indication, he hadn't forgotten.

When she re-entered the bedroom, a team of guards was searching every inch of the room. As if someone might still be there. Inferno was supervising from the doorway, a hand on his earpiece. Leanne was nowhere to be seen but she spotted a pair of sneakers that had likely been left behind for her.

"Are you sure it wasn't a member of your team?" Fiona asked, lacing up the shoes. "Maybe someone on staff who was...I don't know, just checking in on me?"

Inferno looked at her, a lifted brow.

"Maybe someone who forgot to sign off on it and is too embarrassed to come forward?"

That sounded like a nice, safe explanation for what she hoped it actually was. It was so much better than the idea that someone had been standing over her last night, watching her for whatever reason.

"If that's the case then someone will be getting their ass fired."

Fiona wasn't sure she liked that either. If this was a mistake, even though it was scaring the hell out of her now, she didn't want anyone getting fired.

But she also wasn't about to argue with Inferno when he looked as if he was literally about to burst into flames.

"Some of your scales are coming in through your skin."

The tension in Inferno's shoulders suddenly seemed to deflate right out of him. He looked down at his hands, noted the red scales that were there. He reached his fingers up and touched the side of his neck, where more scales were coming in. He grumbled, his hand falling away. "Never mind that." A soft beeping noise came in through his earpiece. He lifted his hand and touched it. "What?" Inferno glanced at her. "Right. Get in here."

Fiona tensed, hearing the door to Inferno's rooms opening up. "What?"

"Sustenance. Eat up, because your day is going to be packed with lessons."

Fiona had tried to object to the use of a food taster with breakfast, but Inferno wasn't going to let her eat before every bit of food was confirmed free of poison. He was done taking any chances. He was going to take every precaution. And he was going to make damn sure that she was equipped with the skills and weapons to fight for her life.

He didn't fire Eric, even though Fiona thought he would. Eric had been off duty during the night; even head guards get to sleep. Eric was as upset about the situation as Inferno was and just as determined to find out what happened.

Inferno took Fiona down to the training grounds that were in another building on the royal property. The building was connected to the palace in two different ways. The main point of entry from the palace was through a long hallway, not quite as elegant as the rest of the open halls inside, but it was bright and gave off a friendly impression that was meant to impress visiting reporters and the occasional tourist for when the palace was open to visitors.

They took that route.

The other way it was accessible was through the basement. Another tunnel-like hallway was thirty feet beneath their feet. Both entry points were used for various reasons. The basement entrance was mostly used to keep the guards in training out of sight of the tourists, but it could also be used should the other entrance ever be compromised. Meaning, if there were ever intruders who had broken into the palace and cut off one of the hallways, there would still be another for them to worry about.

Both tunnels could also be shut down from the palace in case of a fire through various means, but Inferno had always suspected that had only been a feature added in by those who were constantly paranoid about the fate of the royal family.

It was a foolish thing to be fearful of, considering the royal men were required from birth to learn how to fight and defend themselves, and keep up to speed by regularly training with their own bodyguards. For the female royals, it was more of an option, one which only Flare had taken an interest in, that Inferno knew of.

Even if Fiona decided to flee his palace and never return, Inferno wanted her to be armed and able to defend herself. Even then, he might insist on hiring a trainer for her, wherever she ended up, to continue her education.

He still couldn't believe someone had been in the room with her last night. She'd thought it was *him*. She'd been helpless against any attack.

"So, what's going to happen?"

Inferno glanced down at his mate, the woman he wanted to keep with him for the rest of their lives, to bear his children, and he had to look away when he growled. "I'm going to find that fuck and murder him. That's what's going to happen."

"Oh, I meant when we got to the gym."

"Oh." Inferno glanced down at her, and then was forced to look away.

"I thought you were just going to fire him when you found him?"

"If it was indeed an accident and misreporting."

"Right, so, you're not actually going to kill him, are you?"

"Why shouldn't I?"

Fiona stopped so abruptly that Inferno was forced to stop as well. As did the many guards who were following them. Inferno barely saw them. He only had eyes for the woman in front of him, and the way she looked back at him.

It wasn't quite a glare, but she was clearly unhappy with him. "What?"

Her tiny fists clenched. "Are you serious?"

He turned to face her fully, crossing his arms. "We don't have time for this. You're wasting training time."

"Really? Exactly how much time do I have to train here before I leave?"

Inferno couldn't contain his growl. He didn't like the thought of her leaving.

"And now you're growling at me!"

"I am not growling at you," Inferno grumbled.

"Yes, you are. Why? Because I mentioned leaving? What did you think was going to happen when you start threatening to *kill* people?"

"I wouldn't actually kill him. Possibly."

"There! You see? That right there! You can't joke about stuff like that."

"Why not?"

"Because you're *royalty*! How am I supposed to know you're not going to actually do it?"

"Is that what you're worried about? That I would keep my word?"

"In this case? Yes."

Inferno wasn't entirely sure why she was angry about

this. He would have thought knowing someone would have been in her room last night without her permission, or even without cause to secure the rooms, would have been more of a cause for concern.

It must have showed on his face, because Fiona shook her head. "You still don't get it."

"What's not to get?" Inferno threw his hands up into the air. The heat of frustration was boiling over inside him.

"You could get away with killing someone if you wanted to. You could probably make all the people you think of as your enemies vanish and no one would ever notice. That's horrible. Do you even realize that is so much worse than some creep sneaking into my room? I don't care what he was there for, even if he'd tried to attack me. He doesn't deserve to *die* for it, so don't threaten to kill people in my name because I don't fucking like it!"

She yelled those last words, and Inferno was...he was stuck. Rarely had anyone ever gobsmacked him. He'd actually been trained since a small child to keep himself under control, to keep his facial features and body language from appearing confused or shocked, even when he was in the privacy of his own home.

But this had him entirely stunned. He didn't know what to say.

"You're talking about me as if I'm a monster."

She hesitated before speaking her next gut punch. "If the shoe fits."

Inferno couldn't speak after that. He opened his mouth, tried to get the words out that he wanted, but it wasn't working. His throat wouldn't bring forth the sentiments he wanted. He, who was trained to speak, trained to use his voice as well as his strength for the good of his people so he could come across as a confident and articulate ruler...

He couldn't speak.

He looked at Eric, and the other guards, who quickly averted their eyes. Even with the sunglasses on, the tiny tilts of their heads were noticeable as they watched their prince fumble for his words.

Inferno cleared his throat, a humiliation the likes of which he'd never felt before coming over him. He looked to Eric. "Take her to the gym and give her the lessons."

"You aren't coming with me?" She sounded shocked, and Inferno honestly could not tell if it was relief.

"I will be there shortly," he said.

Eric sidled up next to Fiona. "Come, miss," he said softly, pointing his hand down to the end of the hall, as though asking her to lead them.

Fiona looked from Eric to Inferno and back again. Was she wondering if this was a trap? Was she thinking about whether or not Inferno would harm her for not towing the line?

How could she think such horrible things about him after how close they'd been that morning in his bed? Couldn't she see that killing an intruder was just his assurance that he'd do anything to protect her?

He watched her walk away from him, and when she was down the hall, through the doors, and in the presence of multiple men whose jobs it was to die for her if she was in danger.

After the doors were closed, Inferno turned off his earpiece, and then pulled out his phone. He called Ember's number, pleased when his brother answered immediately. "Will you come down here and talk with me? Yeah. I need some help with this."

Before he could find out what was happening to Fiona, and how safe she would be if he sent her back out into the world, he needed to know what his closest and most intelligent family member thought of him and his ability to rule.

Because if his own mate couldn't even see him as anything other than a monster when he was trying to protect her, how could he properly lead the dragon people?

17

"The best confrontation is the sort you can avoid. That being said, if the last case scenario does occur and you're forced to defend yourself, there are some weak points that will help you if you find yourself cornered or held by an attacker."

Fiona liked the trainer Inferno had hired for her. The woman was tough, former military, but human, which meant she could understand Fiona's weaknesses and abilities better than the dragons would.

They repeated some basic moves until Fiona was able to execute them smoothly, without having to think it out. Even so, her mind was on Inferno the whole time, and her eyes kept drifting to the doors, hoping he would show back up. Why was he was so furious with everyone and everything? Was it just his personality? Shouldn't sex have mellowed him out some?

"Good, now stand like this, leg out, perfect. This time, we're going to target your neck. I'm going to put my hands on your neck from behind." The woman stepped up, and hovered her hands a few inches from Fiona's neck.

"No, wait," Fiona stepped away, and turned to look at her. "I don't know I can do that. A few days ago, well—"

"I know about the attack," the trainer put her hands on her hips. "That's why we're doing this. If you work through the trauma with me, then you have a better chance of keeping your wits about you in an attack situation."

Fiona frowned, but nodded. It made sense. She took a breath and stepped back into position.

"I'm not going to choke you, but know that if you do find yourself in this position, you have only about thirty seconds to get out of it."

"Because I'll be dead?" Fiona asked.

"Passed out, on your way to dead."

She swallowed hard. "Does it really only take thirty seconds?"

"Sometimes less. If someone gets the right hold they can cut off the blood flow to your brain and have you passed out in less than ten."

Fiona shivered. She thought about the men who attacked her in her apartment, and the person who was in her room last night. It made her feel vulnerable. Scared. But knowing she had this trainer, and Eric, to help her made her feel stronger.

"I'm ready."

The trainer put firm pressure on her neck, but not enough to hurt her. It still made her feel helpless as she struggled to free herself. She started to wonder if maybe Inferno's anger was because he didn't know how to help her. Maybe he was afraid too.

She didn't even know that much about Inferno. Maybe the threat to people he loved was too real. What if someone had made an attempt on his life at some point, one of his family members? Maybe Inferno had a reason other than just his protective nature to be so angry over this.

Someone could have had their hands on Fiona's throat and choked her to death before she had the chance to do a damned thing about it. Inferno could have walked in that morning and found her dead body.

He was constantly going on about her safety, and yet things seemed to keep happening. That couldn't feel good to a prince who liked to be in control of everything.

"You're going to lose the challenge if you don't find a way out."

Shit. She had to focus. This stuff really could save her life.

When she saw Inferno next, she would have to thank him for this. For everything he was doing as he tried to take care of her.

As hard as she thrashed, or tried to elbow her trainer, or stomp or kick, she couldn't escape. She couldn't pry her fingers off her throat, it felt as if she pulled at a steel clamp. She was just too damned strong for her.

She let her struggle for what had to be way longer than thirty seconds. "I can't do it! You're too damned strong."

"Alright, let's take a break. Go get some water, and then we'll walk through the steps you need to take to break this hold."

Fiona barely took a step away from the mat when Eric was handing her a bottle of water.

"Don't worry about this," he said. "You'll get the hang of it."

"Easy for you to say. You're a dragon. I'm sure training was a breeze"

"Not dragon. Just half."

Fiona blinked. She hadn't expected him to share such information. "Really?"

He nodded. "Yep. From a marriage between a dragon and the Romulus family."

Fiona thought back to the presentation, and the tree with so many pieces blacked out. "They're one of the ones that are no longer around. How is it possible that you're one of them?"

Eric shrugged. "Oh, in the same way that anyone can trace their DNA back to common ancestors, really. One of their descendants broke off at some point, went rogue and married a human, that sort of thing most likely. The rest of my family is normal, not showing any hint of dragon blood, but some recessive gene or another popped up for me."

"And here you are."

"And here I am."

Fiona wanted to ask more. Did that recessive gene that gave him dragon blood give him the ability to shift, to grow scales, or just have super strength? Did he have enough of the genes to marry a dragon and make dragon babies?

They'd have to continue the conversation later though, because her trainer, who liked calling her by her last name, was signaling her. "Blache, break's up, get back on the mat."

The way Ember blinked at him, as if Inferno was speaking a whole other language, wasn't exactly what Inferno wanted from his brother. He growled. "What?"

Ember shook his head. "I just...I mean, I knew you weren't comfortable with the idea of ruling, but are you sure you can make a decision like this?"

Inferno looked away from his brother, and out to the

training building. Fiona was getting the basics, and hopefully she'd gain enough skills to save her own life if he was ever not there for her.

"I can't..."

Ember crossed his arms. "Take your time."

Inferno wanted to growl at him again. Why the hell did Ember have to be so good at stuff like this? He wasn't a pushover either. He had power, strength, could handle himself in a spar with any of the guards, as well as Inferno. Sometimes Inferno lost a battle with him. Sometimes Ember lost a battle against Inferno, and it was the same way with Blaze.

But Ember could keep a clear head, something Inferno couldn't do.

He really should have been the oldest. It wasn't fair sometimes.

"Am I really that fit to rule if I'm so much as thinking about giving it up?"

Ember pressed his lips together, and then he did a little glancing around of his own.

They weren't exactly out in the open, but beneath the shade of one of the smaller weeping willows was hardly privacy. If someone really wanted to, they could listen in on the conversation Inferno was having with his brother and record every word. A task that could also be done if they were inside the palace. There was no such thing as true privacy, not for them.

"I think everyone thinks about it from time to time," Ember said. "Sometimes I'm grateful that I'm not the oldest."

Inferno snorted.

"You don't believe me?"

"Not really. You're exactly the type suited to politics."

Ember grinned at him. "Right. Everyone always says that about someone else."

"But you are."

Ember rolled his eyes. "You sure you're not just trying to convince yourself of that because you want to hand the crown over to someone else?"

"I..." Inferno's defenses suddenly started to rise. "Well why shouldn't I figure out if it's something that would work? If I'm not capable or fit to rule then don't I need to know if one of my brothers can take over if I drop the ball?"

"Fair enough," Ember said, though his eyes were narrowed suspiciously. Inferno didn't like the way he was looking at him.

"What? What are you looking at?"

Ember hesitated, that gleam in his eyes that said he was still thinking about something. "I get it that you're worried for your mate. It's clear she wasn't born ready for this sort of life."

Inner hackles began to rise again. "She's not weak."

"Don't put words into my mouth." Ember full on glared at him. "I didn't say that, but I can tell you're worried about her. You're scared, and to be honest, I don't blame you."

"So then what are we even talking about?"

Ember sighed, looking away from him again, as though collecting his thoughts. When their eyes met, Inferno was left with the impression that he'd done something to severely let his brother down.

"You know, I used to think you were so confident about your role because your strength meant you didn't have to fear any adversary, but I guess finding your mate, and the fact that she is the last of her line, would do this to you."

"Do what?"

"Bring out this weakness, this paranoia, this concern

that you never had for own wellbeing," Ember said. "But don't pull this on me, or on Blaze, unless you are absolutely, positively, one hundred percent sure that you're out. Because I can promise you that I want to be king about as much as you do, and I'm pretty sure Blaze feels the same."

Inferno didn't know what to say. Apologizing seemed like the right thing, but at the same time, not nearly a strong enough gesture for what Ember had just saddled him with.

Or, more accurately, what Inferno just tried to saddle him with.

"I'm not saying we wouldn't step up if we needed to," Ember said. "But right now you're just letting your fears get in the way."

Inferno crossed his arms a little tighter over his chest and pondered his brother's advice. He turned back towards the building where Fiona was. They would still be going over unarmed holds. Would that be good enough if someone tried to smother her with a pillow while she slept? Inferno wasn't sure. He didn't like being unsure, and being a king meant being unsure about absolutely everything for the rest of his life.

"What if she really does not want it? I took her without her permission."

Ember raised a brow. "You suddenly care about that?"

Inferno growled at his brother. "You're getting a little too close to putting your throat on my claws."

Ember clapped him on the shoulder. "Give things time to work out. You made the best decision for her safety, and she's still trying to wrap her mind around everything that's happening. And if the rumors are true, the two of you are already well on the way to creating your lasting mating bond."

Inferno swung on his brother. Ember gracefully ducked

out of the line of fire before turning and walking off. As if they hadn't spoken at all. Anyone who saw either of them right now wouldn't know the depth of the conversation they'd just had based on body language, that was for damned sure.

He might as well look in on what his mate was doing.

He was thinking of giving up the throne? For that *imposter*?

A heat unlike anything ever felt before was nearly blinding, suffocating even. It was insulting to the highest degree.

This would not stand.

18

Fiona was sweating like a pig. Not the kind of sweating she'd seen actresses in movies do where their makeup was perfectly applied and someone had misted them down so their skin was glossy and wet before yelling *action* either.

No. Definitely sweating like a pig. Did pigs sweat? Who cared, because she was using the analogy anyway. She did not look cute when she was sweating. She looked gross.

She grabbed onto her knees, bent over, huffing and puffing for breath, and actually felt the sweat rolling down her forehead and nose. It made tiny dark splashes on the mats beneath her feet, not to mention her boobs felt like they were swimming, squished into her sports bra. She really wanted a nice soak and some clean clothes after this.

So, of course Inferno finally chose to show up, when she was looking her worst, just as Fiona's gut gave up the fight and she vomited all over the gym mats.

Inferno rushed to her side, his large hands touching Fiona's waist and back, as though getting ready to scoop her up and pull her away from the mess.

Nope. She wasn't done. Fiona threw up again.

With the crown prince of all dragons standing next to her. She was making the air he was breathing smell like warm, acidic, half-digested food. Somehow, he was still touching her gross, sweaty body.

"Call for a medic! I want a poison expert in here!"

"She hasn't been poisoned," Eric said, going to open the windows to get in some fresh air, while directing another guard to grab a cleanup bucket and mop.

"I'm just a little hot," Fiona managed to tell him, catching her breath.

Inferno growled and looked at the trainer. "I thought you knew what you were doing. She's a human, she's not supposed to be overworked."

"I wasn't informed that she would have worked out before seeing me."

"She didn't—" Fiona hushed him with a hand on his arm, and his eyes turned wide in recognition. Sex might not be a traditional workout, but it surely had gotten both their heart rates up for a good amount of time.

"I just want to get cleaned up," she told him.

Inferno rubbed her back. If he was at all grossed out by the sweat and vomit, he didn't show it. "We'll get you cleaned up."

"You called for a medic, your highness?" A guard appeared with a first aid kit.

"Yeah," he stood up and let the medic come close to examine her "She might just need some fluid and electrolytes, a little rest maybe."

If Inferno had his way, he would have carried Fiona back to

his room and run the bath for her. Instead, he let her walk, as she requested, and gave her the space she needed to clean up. Sshe'd downed a powerdrink and taken a few extras with her into the bathroom while she showered.

He used the time waiting for her to order food and to call around to check on the investigations into the attack, the green goo, and the intruder. He kept his fury controlled though, not wanting to storm off every time he thought about the danger she could be in, but he wanted to get over to the gun range soon. Knowing his mate was armed and knew how to use the weapon would make him feel a bit more at ease.

When Fiona finally joined him at his small table in the sitting room, the taster had already done his job and left them to their unpoisoned meal.

"You look happy," he commented.

"Leanne left me a large assortment of clothes to choose from. It's amazing how good it feels to have even that much control of your life, after, well, all this," Fiona motioned her arm around the room.

Inferno nodded. "Sit, eat." The words were no sooner out of his mouth than she was devouring the little sandwiches and cut-up veggies.

"Did you figure anything out about who was in the room last night?" She didn't look up at him when she asked it.

"Not yet, but I will."

"Is that you really being confident? Or are you trying not to freak me out?"

"To be honest, it's a little of both."

"Oh."

"What's the smile for?"

She shrugged. "You know, for a guy who kidnapped me, you can be pretty sweet when you want to be."

"Hmm, are we still saying that I kidnapped you? I did have good intentions, if you remember."

"Yeah, you're right. If you're not going to laugh at me for being disgusting and puking twice in the few days that you've known me, then I should stop calling you a kidnapper. If someone's trying to kill me, it seems like the better choice to be whisked away by dragon royalty."

Inferno actually sighed, feeling a weight removed from his shoulders. "I'm so glad to hear you say that."

"I was a little harsh on you, wasn't I?"

"Just a touch, but I may have earned it."

"Yeah, but you've been pretty good to me, too." The sex was definitely nice. He had to push the memories of it out of his head before his body warmed up too much.

"Hardly. Nothing but bad luck has been happening since you arrived, and the one who entered your room last night —" Inferno looked away from her, feeling his neck and jaw tightening as he tried to suck those words back. Too late. They were out in the open now.

"I can handle being reminded of it. I can handle talking about it. You don't have to pretend it didn't happen, or shield me from what's being done about it." Though even as she said those words, she shivered.

"Fiona, I spoke to my brother about you."

She tensed. "You're not, uh, planning on handing me over to him as part of some weird trade, are you?"

"What? No!" Inferno realized there was a lot she still needed to learn about dragons if that was what she thought of them.

"Okay, so what were you talking to him about?"

"Were you serious just now? You thought I would want to hand you over to my brother when you're *my* mate?"

"Well, I don't know how this mating thing works. I've never been mated before."

"Because there's not going to be anyone else." Inferno wanted to keep going, but stopped himself from saying anything else; he didn't want to push his luck.

"Okay, so what did you want to talk about? What did you say to your brother?" She'd stopped eating and turned her full attention on him.

He didn't have a chance to answer, however, because a feminine-sounding shriek interrupted their conversation.

Inferno immediately got to his feet and headed to the front door to his apartment. "What the hell?" He knew that the noise had come from Charrling, and it sounded again, even louder, once he opened his door. He looked to the guards. Eric was speaking into his coms device, but had no answer for him.

Inferno started to run.

19

———

Fiona followed Inferno until she was stopped by a guard as she turned down, what she assumed was, Charrling's apartment wing. "Let me pass. I'm following Inferno."

"Can't do that. Princess Charrling's orders are that she doesn't want you around her or her daughter's apartments."

Fiona took a step back. She supposed she should respect their wishes, but she was still alarmed by the screams they'd heard. "I should be with my future husband and his family if there is something going on."

"Everything is fine. We just got word."

That calmed her down a little. "Okay, great, so what's going on?" If she couldn't see it for herself, then one of these guys needed to tell her.

"It's nothing you need to worry about, just some family trouble."

That was definitely not as specific as Fiona had been hoping for. She opened her mouth to get more information, but then another heavy, tonsil-smacking shriek pulsed through the halls as if a banshee had been released.

Fiona got the chance to see for herself what was up when, from around the corner, Inferno appeared again. Joseph, Charrling's main bodyguard, was also there, and both men held their arms raised up while Charrling stormed towards them in a yellow sparkling gown so fine she could have been getting ready to attend a grand wedding. She swatted at them with what looked to be a rolled up magazine, as though punishing dogs.

"Stay away from me the both of you!" she shrieked, swinging heavily at both men, who were taller and broader, and clearly allowing her to strike at them so as to not hurt her.

Fiona noted how uncomfortable all the guards looked. Her own, Inferno's, and even Charrling's all seemed like they didn't know what to do with the scene. They were torn between protecting their Crown Prince, and letting one of the ladies of the house do...whatever it was she was doing.

Inferno kept his hands raised as he was pelted again and again with the paper, though he sounded angrier by the minute. "Charrling, just calm down!"

"Don't you tell me to be calm! And you! You filthy creep!" She turned her wrath to Joseph, her arm flying up and down as she struck again and again with the paper. If she flapped any harder, she would fly.

"Holy shit, what's going on?"

Fiona turned. Flare and Blaze appeared, and their eyes bulged at the scene as Charrling hit and cursed at Joseph, as if he was a dog who had just pissed on her fifty-thousand-dollar rug instead of the man in charge of her safety.

Or her lover.

"Fiona?" Flare asked.

Fiona briefly looked to the other woman, and then to Charrling. Her perfectly styled hair was beginning to fall, strands coming loose from the heavy layer of hairspray that had kept it done up and braided. It also looked as if there had been tiny flowers in her hair at one point. Either that or she'd crashed into a flower vase and some of those petals stuck in her hair were just collateral damage.

Fiona shook her head. "I have no idea what's going on."

As though signaled by some unseen force, Charrling suddenly stopped striking at Joseph. Not that she'd been doing much damage anyway, but it was beyond strange to see her spine stiffen, and then she suddenly turned quiet. Charrling snapped her head to the side, her blue eyes cold enough to steam the air around her as she pointed her sharp, manicured finger at Fiona and marched forward. "You!"

Fiona stumbled back, her gaze honing in like a laser onto the way Charrling's mean fingernails turned into actual claws. The weird part was how they kept their coloring, and the little jewels that had been glued on didn't fall off. The prettiest deadly set of claws that were about to sink into her throat.

The many guards already around her stepped forward, creating an instant wall between Fiona and Charrling, who shrieked. The guards didn't touch her, but stood shoulder to shoulder as if they were locked into place. Charrling shrieked at them, punching their chests and slapping a few of them in the face.

"Don't touch me! Get out of my way! *You're hurting me!*"

Was she crazy?

"What the hell?" Fiona could barely suck back a breath. She jumped when someone tugged at her wrist, pulling her back.

It was Blaze, his eyes intense. "I think we should get you somewhere safe."

Fiona glanced back, peeking between the guards to see Charrling sink to her knees, as if all the energy in the world had been sapped out of her.

Joseph rushed behind Charrling. He stood over her, his hands reached out, but just barely, as if he wanted to touch her but then didn't dare break the facade that he was just her personal bodyguard. He pulled his hands back and stood straight. Only then did Fiona notice the red lines down his face. He'd been scratched. Badly. Fiona didn't have to think hard to know where those had come from.

Inferno, on the other hand, stood next to Joseph with a less than impressed look in his face. He flat out glared down at her, his huge arms crossed over his massive chest. There was a fire in his eyes, as if he wanted to fight someone, but couldn't because, well, this was his *aunt*.

"What's happening?" This time the voice was Tinder's. She stood next to Flare, dressed in a blue gown almost as bright and flashy as her mother's, trying to peer around the guards.

Inferno growled. "Tinder, just...stay over there and let us deal with this for now."

"*What are you doing*?" Tinder looked at Fiona in much the same way her mother had, but when she stormed forward, it wasn't in Fiona's direction.

She went to her mother.

The guards let Tinder through. Probably because she didn't come out swinging, though they still watched her as she fell to her knees, wrapping her arms around her mother's shoulders, as though Tinder was comforting a woman on death row.

Tinder glared the nastiest look up at Inferno. "You did this! You ruined everything!"

Inferno's eyes flashed. He growled again, this time

showing off the whites of his fangs. He leaned down, his large body menacing, even to Fiona, who wasn't the object of his anger.

"I *don't* care, Tinder. I don't care what her problem is, or what your problem is. I am not mating with you. I will *never* mate with you, and I don't owe you or your fucking mother shit."

Fiona shivered.

"Jesus," Flare whispered softly.

Blaze didn't say anything for a moment, and Fiona thought he might actually be speechless.

Fiona was. These people were his family. Fiona didn't have much love lost for Charrling, but seeing him talk like that, even to defend her...

"Are we clear, Tinder?"

Fiona couldn't see the other woman that well, but she heard the soft, pitiful noise that came from her throat. Then the swing of her hand before the crack of her palm echoed down the hall.

Inferno didn't move, as if her slap had barely fazed him. As if she meant nothing to him. The aura that surrounded him was the sort of *zero fucks given* vibe that even had Fiona scared of him.

Inferno already stood tall, but something about him changed in that next instant. It was as if he got two inches taller, his voice changing, becoming more commanding to the people around him. "Take Charrling back to her rooms. Tinder can go with her, or to her own rooms. It's up to her."

"Yes, sire." Joseph stepped forward, as if he was getting ready to carry out the command.

"*Not you*," Inferno snapped, glaring at the man and halting him in his tracks.

Joseph didn't appear afraid. He and Inferno were close

to the same size, but his expression was clearly shocked. "Sire?"

"Until I know why she put those on your face, you're not going near her." He pointed at the slashes down Joseph's forehead and cheek, which had now started to bleed. Bright red drops formed, making the red look so much more prominent as it slowly bled open. "Blaze and Ember will meet up with you, and you're going to write a complete report on just what the fuck was happening just now, aren't you?"

Joseph's cheek tightened, but he nodded. "Yes, sire."

Inferno nodded, though it sounded more like he just let out a huffing sound before he turned to the others. "Go. Now."

"I am not a prisoner in my own home!" Charrling shrieked, coming back to life in a way that made Fiona want to back up.

"You attacked my mate and your future queen," Inferno said. "This is no longer your home."

Even though Fiona couldn't see Charrling's face from this angle, Fiona could sense the shock around her. As if a cold chill had suddenly formed an icy bubble all around her.

She sputtered, at first, then exploded. "You can't do that! I've lived here longer than you've been alive! I practically raised you!"

"And then you attacked my mate because I won't marry Tinder."

"I won't leave!"

"You will." Inferno nodded as though the decision had already been made. He looked down at her and spoke to her as if she wasn't a vital part of his family. "I'll give you the property along the sea. You'll be comfortable there. If you fight me on this then you won't get even that," he added quickly, as if she had been about to say something.

Inferno turned away from her, addressing the men in suits once more. "Take her away. I need to see to this."

There was a collective nod amongst the guards, a few "yes sire's", and they got to work, like the good little pawns that they were, apparently. Inferno stepped around them, ignoring the hateful glare from his aunt and cousin as he walked to Fiona.

"Quiet now, sweet," he rumbled into her ear, pulling her along, away from his family.

Fiona had to shake herself out of it. "W-wait, what? Why? What are you—"

"No more words. These walls have ears."

She blinked, then understood, or she *thought* she did. It was hard to understand anything around here when there were people who wanted to hurt, and possibly kill, her.

Which gave her the distinct impression that whatever had Inferno acting like this had something to do with Charrling.

Not surprising. That woman clearly wanted to get rid of her, and Fiona was desperate for answers.

"No more words, just come with me."

Fiona nodded. She stuck to it. She didn't say a thing. She let Inferno take her by her hand this time, fingers threading together, and she allowed the dragon prince to march her out of there.

20

———

Fiona entered Inferno's bedroom, or *their* bedroom, as he'd wanted to call it. He'd released her hand only after shutting and locking the door, leaving the guards in the hall and him and his mate inside alone.

She didn't know what was going on, but she was starting to absorb the fact that life as she knew it was completely changed. The fact that he'd called her his *future queen* solidified it.

Queens did not run bakeries.

Fiona folded her arms, watching as the dragon prince grumbled and began sliding his hands all around the furniture in the room. He crouched down to check beneath the tables and desks. When he grabbed a chair to reach up and check the light fixtures on the ceiling, that was when she'd had enough.

"What are you doing?"

"Looking."

"Looking for the ears in the walls?"

He smiled at her, as though pleased she'd understood. "Something like that."

The smile didn't last long before it melted away. He dropped back to the floor, placing his seat back behind the desk where he'd gotten it. "Charrling attacked Joseph for a reason, and now she's flipping out like this...there's got to be more."

"More to what?" Fiona didn't understand and she was getting tired of this. "She hates me because now you're not going to marry your cousin."

"That's not all it is. I know she's hiding something."

Everything seemed so much simpler when her biggest problem was making sure her boss didn't steal her secret recipes.

Inferno went to search around the bedroom where they'd made love not so long ago. That seemed a lifetime ago. She could barely remember it with all the drama she was being forced to swallow.

He came back out, barely sparing her a glance as he marched over to the fireplace.

Fiona blinked wide when he got *into* the fireplace. "What are you doing?"

"Checking." He pushed something out of the way.

She heard the heavy scrape of stone over stone, and Fiona's curiosity got the better of her. It consumed her need to understand what was happening, so she wandered up behind him to have a look just as he ducked into the small space he'd created.

He had to crouch down just to get inside. Fiona could almost walk right in there without ducking at all.

She tried it. The roof of the little passageway he'd created touched the very top of her head, so she had to bend her knees a little. "What is...this is the passage *he* used to get in, right?"

There was no need for Inferno to ask who he was.

Definitely the man who'd wandered into the bedroom where she'd slept, alone, and had stared at her in her sleep.

"If we can find anything that indicates it has been used lately, than yeah, most likely this is how he got in."

Lights flashed on. Fiona blinked. She didn't know what she'd expected to see. Maybe torches lining the stone walls stretching down the narrow corridor.

No. It was actual LED lights spaced out every thirty feet or so. It was shockingly bright in here. There weren't any dark patches where anyone could hide. Fiona suddenly imagined some weirdo lurking in the shadows with a knife or something, waiting to spring.

Nope. It was gray and plain, and she could hardly get horrific nightmares over the sight of this place.

"Is there a way to lock the portal?" she asked. "From our side? So he can't get back in again?"

Inferno made a soft growling noise in the back of his throat, then he answered. "Yeah. We can lock it."

She glared at the back of his head. "What aren't you telling me?"

He turned, looked at her, then shook his head, a grin on his face that she definitely knew the meaning of. "I'll tell you later. Let's get out of here."

"Why?" Fiona drew out the length of that word. The feeling of suspense tingled on her senses. A lot.

Inferno stepped forward. Even hunched over, he was intimidating, and his body radiated sexual heat. "Because it's not very romantic in here."

Fiona backed up, and it would be a total lie if she told herself this was having no effect. Her body tightened, and her sex throbbed with all the potential in his eyes.

"Romantic, huh? After you kicked your aunt out of the

palace and went to investigate the creepy tunnel leading out of your room?"

"It's hardly creepy in here."

He was right. It wasn't even damp, but that wasn't the point.

A softer light washed over her when she stepped out of the fireplace. Inferno stood tall as he followed her. He reached back, pressing his thumb into a single black stone in the fireplace that was arched so it could almost be in the shape of a claw.

She got it. *Blackclaw*. Clever.

Except then he pressed down on another stone, a little diamond shaped one immediately beneath it, and Fiona heard the heavy click that followed.

"There. Locked. See?"

"Great," Fiona said, swallowing hard. "And I can still get out if I need to? Like, I'm not trapped in here if someone tries to bust down the door when you're not around, right?"

She imagined something like that would be set to his thumb print or something, which would be hugely inconvenient for her.

As though reading her mind, Inferno reached out and took Fiona by her hand. "Here," he said, putting her finger to the black claw. He pressed her finger to it. There was a shift and another heavy clicking noise, as though the tunnel was trying to open for her but couldn't. "Still locked. So you press this one first." He made her touch the diamond-shaped stone, and then another click sounded before he brought her finger back to the claw. The tunnel opened for her again. "That's how you unlock it and open it. To close it and lock it is the same thing."

Fiona swallowed. She nodded. She was paying attention. It wasn't like she wasn't, but she couldn't simply ignore the strength and heat of Inferno's hand around her wrist, holding her tightly.

More than once she'd thought his namesake more than fit everything about him, the heat of his body, his personality, everything.

"Understand?"

"Yeah," she croaked, quickly clearing her throat as if that would erase the high-pitched sound she'd just made. "I understand."

Smooth. Real smooth.

She didn't have to look up at Inferno to know he was smirking at her. His thumb stroked across the top of her hand. Still holding her close, he brought her arms forward. She found herself with her hands pressed against her chest, his arms around her, his body spooning up behind her.

So close. So intimate.

His mouth came down close to her ear. She felt the soft brush of his trimmed beard against her skin. "I never wanted this for you."

Her heart lurched. "This what? The drama with your family? Someone trying to kill me? Or at the very least mutilate me?"

He kissed the side of her face that had been burned.

"Yeah, those things."

"Even if I leave, even if I move to a new city and change my name, I'll never be safe again, will I?"

The guilty look on his face said it all before he could open his mouth, and Fiona shook her head, turning away from him.

"I am so sorry."

"Right."

"I'll make it up to you. I promise."

Her heart sank. She was homesick. She was tired. She was so many things right now.

Then, all of a sudden, she was cold as Inferno pulled away from her.

She looked up at him; his guilty expression was still there. "I'll leave you alone for a little while." He turned and walked away from her. She blinked at the sight of his retreating back. Something about that didn't sit well with her. A prince should not be retreating. He shouldn't be the one to leave her alone when he was, at least in part, the reason why she felt this way.

She ran after him, reaching out, snatching his wrist just as he settled his hand on the doorknob.

He looked at her, shocked.

She stared back up at him, no clue what she was supposed to say. Fiona swallowed. God, her fingers didn't even reach halfway around his entire wrist. Why was that something she had to notice right now? "You should stay."

He lifted a brow at her. "I should?"

She nodded, feeling a little more bravery rushing up to greet her. "Yeah, you should."

His eyes flashed. He didn't exactly smile at her, but it was in his eyes. He pulled his hand away from the doorknob. "If you want me to stay, then I will." He reached for her.

She didn't exactly fall into his arms, but it was pretty close to that as she pushed herself up onto her toes and he leaned down, his mouth covering hers in a searing kiss.

Yes, he was going to make this up to her. He could start by making her forget all about how crazy her life had become ever since she'd woken up in his palace.

21

The taste of her mouth was sweet.

Inferno just wished that sweetness wasn't mixed in with the guilt he felt over what he'd done to her. He was a bastard, and she was right to hate him. Whatever this gift was, he was going to take it and be grateful for it. Even if this turned into the last time he made love to her because she was simply taking what she needed from him before ignoring him forever, like a starved dog, he would snatch at it without reservation.

He held her face to his, probing at the sweetness of her lips before she parted for him, allowing him to sink deeply inside that warm, wet mouth that he wanted to claim.

His. His and no one else's.

He backed his mate up to the sofa in front of the fireplace. The bed was too damned far away for him to bother with. He followed her down, cursing his clumsiness as he fumbled in his attempts to get their clothes off. His desire to be with her fueled him along, but a part of him felt a vulnerability he thought he left behind a long time ago.

This woman, this baker, this survivor, was someone he

needed as much as he needed air. They could talk about her leaving all they wanted to, but he knew he would never go a day of his life without her as long as they both breathed. He would give up his birthright just to be near her. He tried to tell her that with his mouth, with his kiss, as they pushed themselves to a more comfortable position on the loveseat.

Part of him thought he should turn the fireplace on for the mood, but that would involve taking one of his hands off her breasts, and he didn't think he was going to be capable of doing that. If he wasn't touching her, then he wasn't breathing.

Her body was scorching to the touch. Her fingers danced in his hair, threading through the strands and gripping tightly. As though a small part of her was allowing her own animalistic side to emerge.

No. Not simply that. She was allowing herself to feed off his energy. Just the way an Istavan should when in bed with her mate.

Inferno growled as he kissed her exposed skin. He made an attempt at being suave and purposeful in his kissing and stroking. He wanted to worship every inch of her skin, leaving her searing as he moved down between her pert breasts, the flat of her stomach, feeling the peach fuzz on her skin darken and thicken as he made it down to her pubic region.

He put all of his attention on her sex, bringing his hand up for a firm stroke between the folds of her. Fiona groaned, a powerful shiver passing through her entire body.

He smiled at her, keeping a firm grip on her thighs as he held them apart before leaning in. He barely allowed his lips to touch her, though he flicked his tongue out, barely allowing it to enter her as he watched her expression carefully.

The color in her cheeks seemed to increase. She brought a hand up to cover her mouth as she struggled to keep those pretty green eyes focused on him.

"Keep your eyes open. I want you to watch me," Inferno commanded. "If you're not watching me, then I'll pull away."

Fiona shook her head, but to his relief, it wasn't because she was denying his command. "Y-you're too embarrassing."

"Embarrassing or no, make sure you're watching this," he said, and then open mouth kissed her wetness, tasting her sweetness, delighting in her moan, her shiver, the way her body clenched around his tongue.

But when she threw her head back in ecstasy, even though his cock throbbed at the sight of her, he pulled back. "I said don't look away from me."

Fiona's perfect breasts heaved. Her brows drew together in a watery glare. "You're a bastard."

"That's true, but this is the kind of bastard behavior you like."

She hardly appeared impressed by this, but it didn't matter. He could tell he had her. He had her, and it was fucking wonderful.

"All right." Fiona spoke with her teeth clenched, and an expression on her face that suggested she was about to crack her molars.

"All right, what?" Inferno leaned down, letting his mouth rest against her pussy lips, but he did nothing else except enjoy the scent of her, and the little shivers of pleasure she couldn't contain.

"All right, I'm looking at you."

"Ah, but you didn't say *please*."

Her green eyes flashed. "I will hit you. I swear I will, and

I don't care if you throw me into your deepest, darkest dungeon for doing it!"

"You don't honestly think I would throw you into the dungeon."

She jerked back a little. "There's an actual dungeon?"

"Of course there is. Every palace has one." He decided to leave it to her whether or not she thought he was being sarcastic or not, because all he wanted to do was get back to her, making her moan his name as he made love to her with his mouth.

She did well to keep her eyes on him this time as he pleasured her, her fingers gripping tighter and tighter in his hair. She was going to leave him prematurely bald, but it was worth it to taste her sweetness, to flick his tongue deep inside her and lifted to her groans.

Inferno couldn't help himself. He began thrusting against the cushions of the loveseat beneath him, desperate for the friction as his erection pulsed painfully, more and more difficult to contain as the sounds of her pleasure had long since gone to his head.

Both of his heads.

He could do this for hours, had he not already desperately wanted her.

"Inferno," Fiona panted for breath. "*Don't stop.*"

More than once he was aware of how she'd turned her attention away from him. How she arched those beautiful breasts and her pebbled nipples to the ceiling, her eyes no longer on him.

He could hardly bring himself to punish her for it now.

Though he was finished punishing himself. He pulled his mouth away from her sex, freeing his cock quickly as he climbed her body.

"N-no," she begged.

"I'm not stopping," he said, kissing her on the mouth, letting her taste herself, and his passion for her. His devotion and love. "I'm giving us what we both need now."

He was a dragon and a prince and a billionaire, powerful, arrogant at times, but still a man.

Inferno plunged inside her.

Tight. Hot. *Wet.*

Inferno nearly imploded right then and there. It was a hard force he could barely contain, and God, if he was feeling this, he was going to make sure she did, too. If this was something he was going to be thinking about for the rest of his life, she was going to think about it. If he couldn't have her out of his mind, then he was never going to be out of hers.

He arched his pelvis, pushing deeper inside, until they were fitting perfectly against each other and he was as deep as he could go.

Fiona moaned wildly before he had the chance to really move. "Inferno, *harder.*"

That was the green light he waited for.

His engines already revved, Inferno slammed his foot on the gas, pedal to the metal, as though he was in the middle of a street race to the finish. Only this was the sort of race he wouldn't mind getting second place in as he slammed into his mate again and again.

Fiona's arms came around his shoulders, she held on tight, turning her head from side to side, as though trying to contain the pleasure in any way she possibly could.

And then something seemed to click for her. She opened those shining emerald eyes wide and just looked at him. Whatever place of Zen she'd fallen into, with that single look, he joined her.

The pleasure still took up the majority of the focus of his

brain, which was to be expected, but then the rest of his focus, which should have been powering the thrusting of his hips, was taken over so he could just...look at her.

His body moved on autopilot, and in that moment, she really was the most beautiful woman in the world.

The woman who would bear his children if she would let it happen. The woman who would be his undoing.

Who could make a prince turn away from his crown.

And he would do it for her, too.

But right then it was all about fucking into her as hard and fast as he possibly could to draw out her orgasm. When her sex clenched tightly around his cock, he knew he had her as she threw her head back and moaned.

"Look at me." He commanded. She did, and it was the look in her eyes through the haze of her pleasure that did him in. Inferno grunted as he felt himself reaching that peak.

"Come inside me. I want you to."

How could he deny such a beautiful, breathy request?

Fiona moaned when he spilled inside her, as though that alone was enough to give her the pleasure she ached for.

Inferno's toes curled. He slammed his hips harder still inside her as he milked the last of his pleasure, satisfying himself because it was his mate he was doing this with.

None other had been able to do this to him, and Fiona didn't even try. That was the craziness of it all.

He slumped onto her, as though all the strength from his body had been drained. Inferno knew he shouldn't be putting all of his weight onto Fiona, but she hardly seemed to mind as she threaded her fingers through his hair again and again.

It felt nice. Soothing.

He felt as though he should be kissing her. He wanted to kiss her. He wanted to make love to her again. He pushed himself up, looked into her eyes, and could see that she wanted the same thing when she bit her plump lower lip.

So why were they hesitating?

Fiona's already pink cheeks darkened beneath his stare. "Wh-what's the matter?"

Inferno could still hear the rush of her heartbeat. Her sex continued to clench and unclench around his cock as her orgasm came down off that sweet pinnacle.

"I'll give it up. For you."

She blinked, her breasts still rising and falling in rapid succession as she caught her breath. "What?"

"The title. This palace. All of it. I don't need any of it." He touched her still healing face. Someone had done this to her because of his title, because of what they were to each other.

Take the title away, and they would be free.

He saw it in her eyes the moment she came to an understanding of what he meant. He was stunned when Fiona shook her head. "You can't do that."

"I can and I will. I will keep my promise. You want a bakery? I'll give it to you. You want a normal life without having to worry about all this bullshit? I'll give that to you, too."

"You can't. You can't give something like this up for me. You don't understand!"

"What's not to understand?"

"I'm..." She seemed to struggle for her words. "I'm just normal. I don't care who my ancestors are or how they're connected to the Blackclaws. I'm normal. I'm nobody. You can't give up being a prince for me."

He knew what she meant, but her words still brought an ache to his heart.

"Fiona, sweetheart, you're not nobody. To me, you're the most important woman on the planet. You're already a queen. If my queen wants normalcy, I'll move mountains to give it to her."

22

———

Fiona couldn't argue with that sentiment enough.

Move mountains? For her?

Why?

She didn't understand why Inferno, a dragon prince with everything at his feet, would be willing to throw it all away for her and her dumb little dream of running a bakery.

What was a bakery when compared to an entire kingdom?

Give that up? For her?

"No."

He nodded, his eyes still dancing. His grin still eager. "Yes." He kissed her. His mouth warm and powerful on hers, intoxicating her, leaving her buzzing, and then so much more when he slid down her body.

It left her gasping already, barely able to get the words out. "In-Inferno, you can't."

He grinned up at her, his mouth still trailing kisses down her skin.

Fiona froze beneath that stare, her breath catching. How could Fiona fight against something like that? How could she look Inferno in the eyes and tell him his gift wasn't good enough? He seemed so eager. So ready to throw everything away, like only a man could, who didn't know what the real world was like.

He didn't understand worrying about paying next month's rent. He didn't understand the disappointment of not being able to buy that nice, shiny new thing that he wanted because the fridge was in need of groceries.

He didn't understand sewing the holes in his clothes shut because saving that extra little bit of cash took precedence over a new pair of jeans.

He didn't understand any of it, and he was offering to put himself through that.

Fiona wanted to tell him no, that she couldn't let him do it. She couldn't let him throw away all of this wealth around him just for her. She didn't care about the Istavan name or what it meant for them. It didn't matter if she was the one who was meant to bear him strong children. She didn't care about destiny, or dragon legends. She barely believed the story about the humans who could carry dragon young in the first place.

She couldn't let him do it. She wasn't worth it.

Her first thought was that she should not let him do such a thing, and her second was how good his tongue felt between her legs.

Then she had no more thoughts after that.

Inferno seemed determined to make love to her until her body could handle no more, and Fiona was into it, so of course she let him do as he wished. How could she not be swept away when she was being made love to by a handsome prince?

Aside from whomever it was in the palace who was doing...whatever it was they were doing to her, how could she not allow herself to get lost in his touch, in his eyes, when he looked at her and touched her the way he did? When he whispered promises in her ear that actually sounded sincere?

He had the real romance novel hero thing going, that was for sure.

Fiona didn't expect to just suddenly pass out after her last orgasm.

Well, she wasn't sure if she actually passed out, but it did seem as though she had a gap in her memory when she suddenly jumped wide awake, sitting up in bed.

She definitely didn't remember moving from the sitting room to the bedroom, or falling asleep.

A fire crackled, adding a sort of ambient glow to everything, some of the light reaching her.

It was because of that orange flickering that she raised the blanket to cover her bare breasts. Apparently, even in the post orgasmic haze she was in, the rules of modesty still applied.

"Inferno?"

A thrill of fear hit her when she realized he was not in bed with her.

If someone could get in and out of the room through secret passageways and whatnot, then wouldn't it be a bad idea to leave her alone like this? Her face was still discolored from the burn facial she'd been given.

Fiona slid out of bed, clutching the blanket tightly to her body, contemplating how quickly she could get back into her clothes. Would she have the time if someone suddenly jumped out of the shadows to attack her?

She raised her voice a little without meaning to. "Inferno?"

"I'm here."

Fiona's heart beat at a normal pace again. She exhaled hard. She hadn't even been aware she'd held her breath.

Fiona walked out into the sitting area of Inferno's room.

He was in front of the fire place, his chair pulled close. He had papers in his hand. The light against his face was of course pleasing. He looked good in all light. There was probably never a time when he appeared rough. Maybe when he was doing his training with the palace guards, but even then, she doubted it.

Inferno took one look at her and stood. "Are you all right?"

She nodded. "Yeah, fine. What are you doing over here by yourself?"

He almost made a picture perfect brooding hero. Had it been full dark, the image would have been complete.

"Just going over some papers."

Fiona wasn't sure she liked that. "About..." She couldn't say it. Inferno looked at her, clearly not understanding. "About giving up your kingdom?"

He blinked, then chuckled, his shoulders trembling with each breath. "No. Even I wouldn't have those papers in hand this soon."

She barely held back her sigh. "Good. Then there's still time to talk you out of it."

He looked at her, his expression amused. "You're not going to talk me out of anything."

Fiona's stomach sank as Inferno sat back in his seat. She swallowed hard and stepped up to him. She glanced over his shoulder. The papers he was looking at contained handwriting. The pen on the little round side table next to his chair told her what she already knew. That it was his handwriting.

Fiona pressed her lips together. He'd said he didn't have anything legal written up yet, but he was still moving incredibly fast. "Inferno, please, you can't do this. It's not... it's not right."

He frowned, turning his gaze up to face her. "Why? It's my title. If I don't want it, then I don't want it."

"But you've got all of this." She looked around, gesturing to the space around her.

"A bedroom?"

"A castle. A *palace*. Aren't you worried about leaving that behind?"

"No. Not in the least."

"You seriously want to leave all of this behind so you can live in a small apartment with me?"

"If it came to that, yes. I would. It won't come to that anyway."

Fiona didn't understand. "But, I thought you said..."

Inferno shook his head. "I'll be giving up the crown. I won't be burdening you with a grown broke mate."

"Oh."

Inferno continued to grin at her as he leaned back in his seat. "Were you honestly worried about that?"

"*No.*" It seemed kind of petty that she had been. Fiona didn't want to think of herself as the sort of woman who worried and obsessed over the money she had available to her. She'd lived long enough on very little, and it wasn't as though she'd had the chance to get used to the luxury afforded to her here.

But still...

"Even if you do take money with you, I don't think...will you really be comfortable dating a baker?"

"I won't be dating you. You're mine. You'll be my wife. Crown or no crown, you will still be my queen."

Fiona ignored the warmth in her cheeks. She still wasn't sure how she felt about the Q word. "Okay then, will you be comfortable being a prince who gave up his title to be married to a baker? That's a fairly simple life. It's probably nothing that you would have ever signed up for."

Inferno tilted his head to the side a little. He stood again. He didn't hold the papers in his hands this time. He faced her full on. "Why would you not believe you are worth this?"

"I...never said that."

"No, but it's in everything you say. It's in all the moves you make. All the looks you give me. You don't think you're worth it. Which is unbe-fucking-lievable because you are absolutely everything to me. This thing that's going on inside my palace walls, it's not only going to stop, but I am ready to give you absolutely everything you want. You just have to open your eyes and realize that you are worth every single thing I want to do for you and more."

Fiona felt an honest to God tremble in her knees at those words. She barely managed to hold the sheet over her body. Her fingers quivered and it took everything she had to stay upright and straight.

Inferno's expression became pitying. Fiona's brain was so scrambled she couldn't even make the decision as to whether or not she appreciated the look.

"You don't believe it."

"I never said that."

He gave her another look that suggested she didn't have to say anything. Inferno raised his hands. He cupped her face. He had the kind of strength that could bend steel with some effort, and yet his touch was such a gentle one. She could melt into a puddle at his feet right then and there and be happy to do so.

Inferno kissed her on the mouth. Another one of his

unfair, heart-stopping, body-buzzing kisses that left her wanting so much more than what she was being given.

He pulled back, and when he looked into her eyes, Fiona thought she could see the dragon within them. His face was...different. Some of his red scales formed along the bridge of his nose and the corners of his jaw.

That fire he looked at her with matched his namesake, and Fiona dropped the sheets around her feet. She reached for him just as he lifted her into his arms. Their mouths came together again as Inferno took her back to his bed.

And in that precious time, Fiona let him make love to her. She let herself believe that she really was worth everything he said she was.

When Fiona woke again, her body was sore, but in the most delicious way she could imagine. There was light in the room. Morning had come. The curtains were closed, but sunlight still streamed in through the cracks and the lace.

Fiona turned onto her back, stretching luxuriously, feeling it all the way in her toes before she sighed and turned into Inferno's chest. His hand came up, fingers sliding against the flesh of her back, though his eyes were still closed.

"How are you feeling?"

She smiled against the warmth of his skin, snuggling closer.

She knew what he was talking about. His claws were back in now that the night was over. The scratches he'd left down her back had hurt at the time, but she'd been so into what he was doing that the pain had faded away quickly.

"I'm all right."

Inferno opened his tired eyes, lifting himself up enough to take a look at what he'd left behind on her flesh.

He cursed.

Fiona tensed. "Is it bad?" She didn't exactly feel it now. Not really. How bad could it be?

"Bad enough. I'll get some ointment for you."

He tried to pull out of bed. She grabbed him. "Don't even think about it." Fiona sat up. She could see herself in the mirror on the wall. She half turned. Even with the distance, it didn't look bad. She doubted it would look too terrible up close either. Three red scratch marks. Fiona checked the sheets. There was some spotting there, but that was the extent of it. "This is fine."

"It's hardly fine. You're bleeding."

"Yeah, barely."

"At least let me grab you something for—"

"No." Fiona grabbed Inferno's arm and yanked him back down when he tried getting up again. She knew she would never have the strength to force him to do anything, so he was only accommodating her wishes.

It was amusing that he still did it with a scowl on his face. "Fiona."

She settled next to him, absorbing his warmth and letting herself get comfortable. "Don't *Fiona* me. You can't do what you did last night and not expect me to be in a good mood about it."

His hand settled on her hip. "I suppose."

Fiona smiled. "Just give me another hour. You can mother hen me then."

Inferno sputtered, his hand jerking away. "*Mother hen?*"

Fiona tried not to laugh, but that was pretty much impossible.

Today was going to be a good day.

Until a heavy banging sounded on the door to Inferno's room.

Inferno sighed, then cursed. "Goddammit."

"Don't answer it." Even as she asked, Fiona knew it wasn't that simple.

Even a prince had to answer his door.

Inferno got out of bed. He grabbed his pants, putting one foot at a time in them before heading to the sitting room. He shut the door behind him, hiding Fiona away from the main area where Inferno would be dealing with whoever was banging to get in.

Fiona grabbed the sheets, yanking them over her head and taking Inferno's pillow. It was still warm, so she snuggled it. Not quite the same, but it would do until he came back.

Still, she could make out the voices of the people on the other end of the door when Inferno answered it. His brothers. Both of them. Blaze and Ember came with some fairly important news.

Joseph was confessing to the crime of trying to have Fiona assassinated.

She sat up straight just as Inferno made something crash in the other room.

23

———

Fiona couldn't get herself dressed fast enough, and even then, throwing one of Inferno's oversized bathrobes over her shoulders hardly counted. She rushed out of the bedroom she shared with the dragon prince just to watch him yell and scream in his brothers' faces. Like a giant screaming at two other giants, his face bright with rage.

It took her a minute to see that he wasn't screaming *at* them, but the way he barked his orders and commands was clearly doing something to that vein at the side of his neck.

"I want him interrogated *now*! I want him in front of me with his head in the stocks! I want every single damned thing he has to say—"

Inferno stopped suddenly, as though only just realizing that Fiona was standing there. He and his brothers looked at her, and for a horrible second, Fiona felt incredibly naked. She should have put on more than this bathrobe. It felt a little too much like wearing a tent in front of her mate and his brothers.

Inferno's rage hardly left his face, even as he looked as

though he was trying to rein it in. "Fiona, sweet, I think you should let me handle this."

"I think the whole palace heard you screaming like that."

He glowered at her. "The only person I wanted hearing it was Joseph." He turned back to his brothers. "When do I see him?"

Ember made a half-hearted noise of uncertainty. "I don't know."

"I won't torture him." He seemed to think on that. "Much."

Fiona felt that familiar worry rising within her. "You would torture him?"

Inferno waved his hand at her. "Only so far as he has already tortured you. I might dunk him into that cream and see how long it can sit on his skin before he begs for mercy."

Fiona clenched her teeth. She couldn't tell if he was joking. He had to be joking, right? Inferno was a prince and he did get to do pretty much whatever he wanted, but even royalty had to live by a set of rules.

At least, the royalty she was aware of.

Now that Fiona thought about it, she wasn't sure if she was aware of anything to protect Inferno's citizens from the possibility that he might become a tyrant.

But he wouldn't. Would he? Even to a man who was guilty?

"Don't hurt him."

Fiona noted the sudden tension in Inferno's shoulders. The way he slowly turned his head to look at her with those bewildered eyes was almost enough to make her take back her words. "Don't hurt him? *Him*?"

Fiona's legs itched to back up a step. She almost did it,

almost giving into that look on his face and the tone in his voice.

She held herself firm, steeling her body and clenching her fists. "I don't want to be with a man who tortures people."

"This is different. It would hardly be torture. He would just be inconvenienced for a few hours."

"A few hours being burned the way I was?"

"Just until he bleeds a little. It's not as though I'm talking about pushing his nose inside out with my fists. His face will need to be in proper order when he stands trial."

"If he's going to stand trial then he doesn't need you to do this to him."

Inferno rolled his eyes, a growl leaving his throat as he turned away from her. "You know nothing of this."

Fiona's heart pounded. She wrung her hands together. She'd been so sure they were done with this. That they'd come to an agreement. Or at least were going to meet each other halfway. It seemed as though Inferno hadn't listened to her at all.

"So you're going to put him into a vat of that stuff used on me, and then beat him? What will that solve? He already confessed." Even as Fiona could understand why he wanted to do that, the idea that he would was a little too... She couldn't handle it. She didn't want him to beat anyone, for any reason.

Inferno's brothers looked at her, and then at Inferno. She couldn't read the looks on their faces other than the extreme discomfort.

It seemed too barbaric, but she would never say that word out loud, knowing how much dragons, and shifters in general, tended to despise it.

"Please, just...don't let this get to you."

"*Why not?*"

The outburst did make her fall back a step this time. Fiona couldn't help herself.

"Brother." Ember stepped forward, gripping Inferno's shoulder, but Inferno shrugged the other man off, turning his heated stare back to Fiona.

Inferno looked at her as though she'd gone insane. As though she was the one he didn't understand in this situation. "Do you forget how I found you? Armed, black-clad men came into your home and tried to harm you. Kill you even, all because I looked at you in a way I shouldn't have. One look was all it took for them to know, and had I not been there, had I not been desperate enough to see you, you would be dead. I would never have had the chance to know you. And then your face. He attacked your beautiful face in my home! Under my nose!"

"It's not permanent."

"I do not care!"

His voice shook the walls. Fiona's heart fluttered awkwardly. She couldn't understand this feeling inside her or get control of it. The odd relief that bubbled up, as well as the anxiety that hit her at the same time.

Worse, she didn't entirely know how to articulate why this was getting to her.

"I don't want this to turn you into someone I don't want to sleep next to at night."

That was probably not the way she should have laid that out. Definitely not the best way to put that forward if the wide-eyed stare Inferno was giving her was anything to go by.

"Inferno—"

He raised his hand to her, as though waving her off,

wanting nothing to do with her as he marched out the door. "I need to think."

"Inferno!" She rushed after him. Ember and Blaze stepped in her way before she could make it out the door.

She glared at them, anxiety building within her as Inferno marched away from her. "Get out of my way."

They didn't mention to her how backwards it was for her to be ordering around a couple of princes. Blaze shook his head, looking to his brother for help, and Ember seemed entirely too patient for Fiona's liking.

"If you go out in that, he will kill us."

"Figuratively?"

Ember half rolled his eyes, as though reminding himself he needed to be careful with his words. He looked a little more like Inferno just then.

"Yes, but you know that. He must have had this talk with you by now."

"He did, but he's talking about torturing that guy. You can't just let him do that."

"He's the future king. He can do whatever he wants," Blaze said, though his voice was not unkind as he gave her that sharp little reminder.

"Can I go and see Joseph?"

"That's probably not the best idea in the world right now," Blaze replied.

Ember was clearly trying not to smile. "Yes, especially dressed like that. The press would have a field day with that one."

"I don't know why you pretend to care. If the press do anything you don't like, you could just have them all tortured or killed."

Both princes twisted their noses at her, as though she'd just said something horribly disgusting.

Blaze, usually so playful, seemed the most offended. "Is that what you think of us? We would never do that."

"No, you wouldn't, but you could."

"We would not do that. Why do you want to insist so badly that we're monsters?" Ember asked. His tone was the most patient, and it made raw guilt eat away at Fiona's stomach.

"I don't think you're monsters and I'm not trying to accuse you of anything, it's just...I don't know. It seems wrong for anyone to have the power to do that to someone. To torture someone? One of your own subjects?"

"He's an enemy of the crown and the kingdom for having anything to do with your injuries and the danger you've been put in." Ember put his hand to her shoulder. "This is not a man you should be tying yourself in knots for."

Fiona's hands clenched. "I know."

"Then why bother?" Blaze growled.

Ember glanced back at the man quickly, as though trying to tell him to shut the hell up, but Fiona heard it anyway.

She couldn't quite put her finger on exactly why this was a problem for her.

The Blackclaw family had been ruling this kingdom since its inception. There had been a couple of kings who had gone off their rockers, a few royal murders that people liked to gossip and make conspiracy theories about, but for the last four generations of dragon rulers, almost three hundred years, everything had been peaceful within the borders. Content. No one seemed to mind and the only problems seemed to be the standard political affairs that happened from time to time.

Fiona almost never heard of an innocent man jailed or

tortured after being falsely accused of a horrible crime, and no one minded the laws forbidding hateful speech against the royal family because no one hated the royal family enough to speak ill of them.

She'd never bothered herself with these thoughts before, and yet now...

She looked up at both men in front of her, neither of whom had done anything to warrant accusations.

Inferno had offered to give up everything for her, but these men would still become her brothers. Why enter into a family on such ugly terms? Why bother pulling them into her own doubts when she could hardly articulate them?

"I'm sorry. I was just...I guess I'm a little sensitive about these things."

"But why?"

Ember elbowed his brother in the stomach, glaring at him before returning his attention to Fiona. "Apology accepted. It's an ugly business, and we understand that there would be some hesitation when it comes to this matter. Right, Blaze?"

This time, there was an edge in Ember's voice, and Blaze crossed his arms before reluctantly relenting. "Right. Apology accepted, Fiona."

"Good." Ember nodded, turning back to Fiona. His smile was kind, though Fiona still didn't feel better.

She crossed her arms, suddenly cold. She could hardly bring herself to look at either man now that she'd badly embarrassed herself.

Maybe the thing that made it worse was how patient Ember was being about the whole thing. "I'll bring Flare over here with Eric and a couple of the other guards. You shouldn't be alone right now."

Fiona nodded. "Will Inferno be long?" She almost

wanted to ask them to plead with Inferno not to go too hard on Joseph, but after her little conversation with Inferno, her terrible, stupid, horrible defense of the man Inferno probably hated most in the entire world, she wasn't up for pushing her luck.

"Hard to say, but if he takes too long, I'll give him a gentle push that he will need to come back to you. Maybe he shouldn't be getting his hands dirty with this when he has his mate to come back to."

Fiona looked into Ember's eyes, saw the understanding there, even if he didn't want to give it, and she could have hugged him. "Thank you."

Ember nodded. "Blaze. Stay with her for a moment. I'll get our sister."

"She's got plenty of guards."

"She doesn't need the company of palace guards, fool. She needs family."

Fiona's heart fluttered a little at that. Family. She was already family to these people. The warmth within her struggled against the guilt for having questioned them, but she pushed it aside. The word family. An actual family. Even if some members if it didn't want her or like her, like Charrling and Tinder, she had a family.

That word alone was enough to make her worries about Inferno's revenge, and the power these people had over their subjects, melt away into nothingness. How could she focus on the bad when she knew she wasn't truly alone, and never would be again for the rest of her life?

Of course, her mate was still away, questioning, and probably torturing, Joseph.

Until Inferno came back to her, it would be impossible to not think about that.

24

____

Flare came over with a soft, careful smile and a cloth bag with embroidered flowers under her arm. Eric stood behind her when the woman pulled Fiona into a soft hug.

"Are you okay?"

Fiona pulled back, noting the look on Flare's face, as though she was waiting for something, some kind of outburst.

Right. Her brothers had told her what had happened. Made sense. They were family, after all. Fiona was going to be part of their family, but she had only just arrived. Flare was their baby sister.

"I'm okay. Still waiting to hear when Inferno's coming back."

Something within Flare noticeably eased up, as though the tension had just deflated right out of her pores. "Well, I'm sure he'll be back soon." Flare looked back over her shoulder, and Fiona saw a brief look pass between the two before Flare shut the door. When Flare saw Fiona's curiosity, she turned away, her cheeks reddening at what could almost be a confession.

Fiona couldn't help but smile. A secret romance between a dragon princess and one of the palace guards seemed a little more like the kind of drama Fiona wanted to be part of. Anything but this murderous B-style movie mystery she was stuck living through right now.

Flare looped her arm through Fiona's, heading for the delicate couch in front of the fireplace. "I brought some snacks. We can watch a couple of movies. I brought some goodies. *Baseketball. Super Troopers, Porkies—*"

"Wait, what?" Fiona almost laughed at the titles listed. "You have movies like that here?"

Flare's grin showed off the whites of her teeth. "We sure do." She pulled them out of her bag, showing them off, along with a few other choices.

Fiona shook her head. "I'm stunned."

"And so would the rest of the world be. There's a reason we don't have these on our iTunes accounts or watch them on Netflix. The world has to think we don't have a sense of humor. So for stuff like this, DVDs are the way to go."

Fiona nodded. "Can't be hacked. No one can know you watch them."

Flare winked. "You got it. And I figured we could use a good laugh right about now."

"A laugh, and maybe some breakfast? What do we do, like call down to the kitchen or something?" Fiona made her way to the phone, but Flare beat her to it.

"You get dressed, I'll order breakfast."

Fiona looked down at the bathrobe and remembered her nakedness. "Right."

Flare was right, Fiona felt a lot better after a quick shower, a change of clothes, breakfast (poison tested first, of course), and the first DVD completed. The only thing that would make it better would be if Inferno was there with them.

After a long silence, Flare finally spoke up. "How are you feeling?"

Fiona pressed her lips together. She didn't want to talk about this. She didn't want to make things awkward between herself and her new family.

"Just wishing everything was back to normal. But I guess being mated to your brother means that's never going to happen."

"Well, not even that. I mean, you're already his mate, but once it's all official with the courts and the wedding happens, you'll be a queen."

So Flare didn't yet know that Inferno was planning on giving up the throne.

That was...interesting. Should she tell her? Fiona didn't know what the rules where in a situation like this. It seemed like the sort of thing she should tell her. This was Flare's family. Her brothers. Their lives.

If Inferno really was intent on giving up his throne, then that would impact Blaze as the next in line.

"Actually, Inferno and I were talking about that, and Inferno's decided to give the throne to Blaze."

Flare jerked back a little in her seat. She blinked. "What?"

"Yeah." Fiona cringed a little. "I'm sorry?" She didn't know if she should apologize, but it seemed like the thing to do in that moment.

Flare shook her head, looking away from Fiona.

"Is it really that shocking?"

"I mean...no. I suppose not, but the idea that Inferno won't be king...I always thought he would be..."

Maybe this was another thing that Fiona was never going to understand. For royalty, Fiona imagined things were set in stone from the moment they were born to the moment they died. As each sibling was born, they were born into a hierarchy, knowing that the sibling before them would inherit before they would.

And now it was something that Blaze's children would be born into. Because Fiona didn't want to have two or three kids and have to explain to them that one of them was going to be more powerful than the others. She couldn't imagine how it would feel to be one of the younger ones, knowing that they would get less than the first born.

The realization, one that hit her only then, made her stomach clench.

No one was going to come out on top with this. This was a burden, one that Inferno was giving up because Fiona refused it.

She wanted Inferno. She wanted to be his wife and spend her life with him. But she didn't want his crown and all the drama that came with it, whether that be assassination attempts or people talking trash about her on social media. Only now did Fiona see how selfish that could be.

And the look on Flare's face told her just how much she was muddling up the situation.

Flare opened her mouth, as though to say something, but was cut off by the knock at the door.

A soft knock. Nothing threatening, though Fiona still jumped.

"Who is it?" Flare called, clearly not as put off by the knock as Fiona was.

Eric's voice answered. "Your cousin is requesting an audience with Fiona."

Fiona blinked. Tinder. What was she doing here?

Flare gestured to the door, as though asking whether or not she should answer it.

Fiona was struck helpless with that. What was she supposed to say? No? Tinder was also a member of the royal family, though Fiona had stolen the man she was supposed to be with. Had Inferno not met Fiona, or had even met her a couple of weeks after the wedding, there was no telling how this story would have progressed.

Fiona shrugged and nodded. Despite everything, she couldn't turn the other woman away.

Flare got to her feet and went to the door. She opened it quietly.

Tinder stood on the other end, her face barely concealing her misery. From her spot on the couch, Fiona felt badly for her. Not that she would ever say that. The other woman would probably hate to have any of Fiona's sympathy.

"Tinder, are you all right?" Flare asked.

Tinder shook her head. She came into the room, and Flare shut the door behind her.

Inferno felt something he'd rarely felt since before Fiona came into his life. Something that was becoming all too familiar with him as of late. Something dangerous.

A lack of control.

His hands were barely hands. His fingernails lengthened into points. They were fairly small, but as thin as box cutters and looked even nastier.

He stepped away from Joseph, grabbed the empty chair in the room, and yanked it in front of the other man. He sat down, his arms up on the back end of the chair. He needed a rest almost as much as Joseph did, but for different reasons.

"You're tiring me out. Honestly, I'm impressed with that."

Ember cleared his throat. "Inferno, maybe now is the time to stop."

"It absolutely is not and you can fuck off if that's the stance you're going to take." Though Inferno was positive his brother wasn't just playing good cop to Inferno's bad cop, it was fine anyway. Inferno could still use this to his advantage.

If Joseph bought it.

There was a good chance he wouldn't. The guy was smart. Mostly.

"Why did you do those things to Fiona?"

Joseph's head was ducked. He wouldn't look Inferno in the eyes. The other guards standing around the room, one for each corner of the square holding cell, stood stoically, staring ahead, as though there wasn't a traitor in their midst. Or an interrogation.

"Joseph, I don't want to do this to you anymore than you want me to do it. You think I want to go back to Fiona knowing your blood is beneath my fingernails? Talk to me and this stops."

Joseph said nothing.

That brief slice of patience Inferno had conjured up began slipping through his fingers. He clenched his claws into the steel frame of his chair.

"Joseph, were you working alone or by yourself? If you don't answer me, I'm going to assume you had an accomplice and I *will* go looking for them."

Joseph finally looked up at him, and Inferno knew he'd hit the right mark.

Finally.

"Who is it?"

Joseph shook his head. "There was no one."

Inferno stood. He kicked the chair away. It banged loudly against the wall. His men who were standing there didn't so much as flinch as the metal crashed into the wall. It didn't hit them, thankfully, because Inferno hadn't intended to kick it so hard.

"Inferno, honestly, stop."

Inferno pressed his hands to the arms of the chair where Joseph's wrists were bound. He leaned in close. The thick shackle around his neck would keep him from lunging forward and biting, not that Inferno was concerned too much with that. He couldn't be sure if that was misguided. He'd thought he'd known Joseph. The man had worked within his household for years. Years.

And then this. Out of seemingly nowhere.

Possibly that was why this offended him so much. It wasn't just that he'd gone after Fiona, Inferno's true mate, the only human woman on the planet who could give him children, but it was also that Inferno never in a million years would have looked twice at Joseph.

Never would have suspected him...

"There is someone else. Who? Charrling? I know you've had a sweet spot for her for a while. Do you want me to bring her in here, too? Because I fucking will."

Joseph pulled against the bonds that held him, his eyes flying wide with panic. "You can't do that! She is royal blood!"

Finally. A reaction.

Inferno smiled. An evil seed sprouting within him. "I would."

"Inferno—"

"Shut the fuck up, Ember."

Inferno felt more like a dog than a dragon. There was a drop of blood finally spilled and he was honing in on it.

Ember growled low and dangerous behind him. The hairs on the back of Inferno's neck stood straight up. It took willpower to keep his eyes on his prisoner instead of glancing back. Inferno had never heard such a sound from his brother before. He barely blinked, staring into Joseph's terrified eyes.

Ember wasn't done. "Even if he confesses to anything, at this point, there is no guarantee he will be telling the truth."

"I don't care. Who were you working with, Joseph?"

"This is exactly what your mate was worried about."

Inferno's spine stiffened. He slowly turned back to face his brother, and he was almost as ready to attack him as he was Joseph.

"I'll tell you. I will, just...don't hurt Charrling."

Inferno barely resisted the urge to roll his eyes. Joseph and Ember could both get fucked.

Of course, he wouldn't actually strap his aunt down and do to her what he was doing to Joseph, but these two idiots didn't need to know that. Since, well, if she did have something to do with this, he wasn't making promises.

"Who are you working with? Someone put you up to this?"

Joseph nodded, a tremble in his tense limbs. "It was... Tinder. Tinder had me do it."

25

Fiona stood when Tinder came into the room. It didn't seem right to stay seated before her. She was a member of the royal family, even if she and her mother hated Fiona's guts. Even so, Fiona wanted to hug the other woman to help disperse the misery she might have felt, but there was no way in hell something like that would be welcome.

In fact, when Tinder looked at her, there was a hint of red around her eyes that Fiona hadn't noticed from across the room.

"Are...are you okay?"

Tinder nodded, pressing her lips together. "I wanted to see you."

"Me?" Fiona looked to Flare, as though the other woman would be able to offer some insight.

Flare shrugged helplessly, as though she was as troubled by this whole thing as Fiona was.

Tinder looked to Flare. "Can you leave us be for a moment, cousin?"

Fiona felt a rising tension building from the bottom of

her spine, all the way up into the back of her neck. She couldn't explain it, but she knew in that moment she did not want to be left alone with Tinder.

Fiona realized Flare was the best woman in the world when she reluctantly shook her head. "I don't think that's a good idea right now, cousin."

Tinder closed her eyes, as though struggling for patience. She removed that elegant hat, holding it in front of her. "Please, this is important."

Fiona shook her head. "I'm sure whatever you need to say is something your cousin can hear."

Tinder frowned. This was clearly not something she wanted to hear.

"But hey, I'm sure it's all right." Fiona finally let go of her inhibitions as she put her hand onto Tinder's shoulder. "Are you worried about Joseph?" She knew the man was loyal to Tinder's mother, though she knew better than to mention why. Her mother might be having an affair with the man. That might not be something Tinder wanted shoved in her face.

Unfortunately, even mentioning the man's name was enough to make Tinder's eyes glow. The woman bared her teeth, reminding Fiona that this was still a dragon she was dealing with. Even a poised princess could be dangerous.

Fiona tensed, looking back into those hateful eyes that seemed to want to burn holes through her.

Flare took Tinder by the arm, catching her attention, breaking whatever spell it was that she'd been under. "Tinder, come on, it's time to go."

Tinder jumped at the touch, blinked, and looked away from Fiona. "Y-yes. You're right. I'm sorry."

The only reason Fiona didn't back up a step was because she was trying to not look too disrespectful. The vibe the other woman gave off was just…something else. "Are you sure you're okay?"

Tinder glanced at her before nodding. "Yes. We can speak later."

If they did, Fiona already decided she was going to have Eric or Inferno there with her. There was no way she was going to let herself be alone with the woman who would have been Inferno's wife. Not when she got stared at like that.

Tinder turned away with Flare. They walked back towards the door. Flare opened it, her hand lingering on Tinder's shoulder as the other woman stood in the doorway. As though she was thinking about something.

Flare glanced back at Fiona, as though she was just as confused as Fiona was about the whole thing.

"Tinder? Are you sure you're—hey!"

Fiona felt a heaving jump in her chest when Tinder grabbed Flare around the shoulders and pushed her hard outside of the bedroom, quickly slamming the door shut. Fiona heard the distinct sound of a lock clicking into place, despite the shouts and bangs coming from the other side.

"Whoa, whoa, okay, what are you doing?" Fiona stayed behind the couch, her limbs tense, but she had something between herself and the other woman, so that meant she was all right.

For now.

"They won't be kept out of here for long."

Fiona didn't understand, and as Tinder approached her, Fiona walked around the couch, keeping it between them. "You mean the guards?"

Nothing about Tinder's body posture or language suggested this was some innocent thing, that she *really* just wanted to tell Fiona something important. Not with the way she glared, the way her fists clenched and the whites of her teeth were visible.

"You took *everything* from me."

Okay, so this was definitely going where Fiona had been worried it was going to go.

When Fiona had the door to her back, she lunged for it. "*Eric!*"

Her fingers clenched around the handle of the door, but she didn't get her chance to even try opening it when thin, steely fingers gripped her around the back of her neck, yanking her back.

Fiona went into the air. She didn't understand how that could have happened, but it did. She was flying. She was in the air soaring above Tinder's head, and when she landed with her back on the carved wooden frame of the couch, she screamed even louder as she thought she might have broken her back.

Shouts sounded on the other side of the door. Heavy bangs. Inferno once told her how everything was reinforced for the safety of the royal family, and the secret escape through the fireplace was cut off, so there was no getting out there.

Tinder walked around the couch, and her lovely manicure had lengthened into gnarled claws that Fiona knew were meant for her throat.

"I'm going to kill you, you bitch!"

She had one chance left. She waited for Tinder to get just close enough to her that she could make her move. Recalling everything she'd been told in her brief self-defense lesson, Fiona had perfect balance on the floor, even if she couldn't move. Tinder would have to come to her, and when she did, Fiona prayed her aim was on point as she kicked out her foot, cracking the other woman hard in the knee.

Tinder screamed a murderous noise as she fell back. Hitting a spot like that had the right effect, and while Tinder rolled on the ground, crying and clutching at her knee, Fiona grabbed the side of the couch.

It was amazing how she was able to feel so little of the pain in her lower back when her life was on the line, and she dragged herself to her feet, hurrying with her back hunched over to her and Inferno's bedroom. It was her only choice, as Tinder was between her and the door, but she was confident that she'd be protected in there because it was separated from the sitting room by another door. A reinforced door she could lock.

Fiona made it inside as Tinder dragged herself, red-faced and still screeching, across the floor towards her, as though she was the one being attacked.

Fiona didn't let the other woman get close. She slammed the door, turned the lock, and fell against the wall. Breathing hard, Fiona sank to the floor just as she heard, and felt, Tinder banging with her fists on the other side.

"Go away, you psycho bitch!"

God, her back still hurt, and her heart pounded. That had been a little too close.

"He was supposed to be mine! He loved me first!"

Fiona could shout back to her that Inferno never loved her, that he had to marry her because if he couldn't have his proper mate, one of the Istavan humans, and he needed to make baby dragons with another dragon. She was his cousin, and a member of royal blood. That was the only reason why she'd been chosen. If he had married her, it would have been out of duty and not love.

That seemed a little too cruel to point out, but considering the bitch had tried to kill her, Fiona wasn't entirely above being petty.

"I think he just wanted stronger dragon babies. Since the ones you would have given him would have been *weak*."

The banging and screaming on the other end of the door stopped for a split second before the sound picked up again, the banging twice as strong as it had been before.

The scraping noise made Fiona think the other woman was trying to dig her way through the door with her claws, and her voice sounded anything but human now.

"You bitch! You filthy, petty human! I *hate* you!"

"The feeling's mutual," Fiona muttered, though she doubted Tinder could hear her.

Those people who had broken into her apartment, the burning face cream, the awkward meet-ups...

Tinder had actually tried to kill her.

It was funny because Fiona had been getting ready to put her money down on Charrling.

The shattering sound of the main doors outside made Fiona jump out of her thoughts, and Inferno's terrified voice called out to her, signaling that she'd made it to the end.

She'd survived.

"Fiona!"

26

—

Fiona heard a terrible shrieking noise on the other side of the door. It almost sounded as though Tinder was being murdered out there, but Fiona knew that wasn't the case.

It sounded bad as she screamed, as something that sounded expensive crashed to the floor and several people struggled with her.

"Get her down! Get her down!"

"Get off of me! Get off of me now!"

Fiona felt bad for it, but she was relieved, and kind of glad. The bitch had tried to kill her. Fiona hoped this was scaring the hell out of her.

She was only able to bask in that terrible, vengeful sensation for a few brief seconds before the sound of Inferno's voice, cool and soothing, pulled her out of that dark pit before it could leave its lasting impression on her.

"Fiona!"

God, he was still out there. She unlocked the door and yanked it open, determined to rush out into his arms.

Inferno stopped in front of the door, two feet away from

her. He'd been marching towards it and now he stood there, staring at her as though he couldn't quite believe she was here.

Alive.

Inferno moved before Fiona could break the spell, gathering her up and pulling her hard against his stony chest. She felt his relieved sigh, and a rumble within his chest, the sort that reminded Fiona of a kind of release. All the tension, anxiety, and fear he'd felt steamed out of him now that he could let it go.

That he had been that worried about her made her even more grateful to have him. Especially right now. "I'm all right."

It was as though he was absorbing any lingering fears like a sponge. She felt nothing but relief.

Inferno said nothing right away. His fingers laced into her hair, his other hand sliding down and around her waist. He touched her shoulders, her arms, and Fiona realized just then that he was patting her down, searching for some hint of a wound.

She grabbed his hands, stopping him. "I said I was fine."

Inferno stared at her, and she'd never seen his complexion so pale. Even with all the scary moments she'd had after coming into his palace, even with everything she'd found out about him, she'd never once seen him like this.

"Are you okay?" Fiona looked into his eyes, searching for any hint that he was at least awake in some sense. "Inferno?"

He nodded, finally showing her that he was at least paying attention. "I thought I would be too late."

Fiona's heart did a backflip somersault sort of thing that would have made a professional cheerleading team proud. Heat suddenly burned in her eyes and the sound of Inferno's voice, and the look on his face, made her want to cry.

She wrapped her arms tightly around him, holding him close and trying to center herself.

Which was difficult because she could still hear Tinder screaming as she was being yanked out the door.

"I didn't know it was her."

Fiona nodded. "I believe you."

From outside Inferno's living quarters, Fiona heard Flare calling out, demanding to know what was going on, if Fiona was all right, and most likely being as disruptive as possible. Fiona's appreciation and affection for the other women grew about a thousand percent in that moment.

But then another long, high-pitched shriek soared brokenly through the palace. Fiona figured people off the property and on the closest street might be able to hear it as it made her eardrums flutter.

Inferno yanked Fiona behind him, his body tense as he took a defensive stance. The guards outside their room shouted. Someone screamed as though in pain.

"What's happening?" She didn't need to ask. Fiona already had an idea of what was going on.

Inferno didn't glance back. "Stay behind me."

Fiona did as she was told, but she also could not stop herself from peeking around his shoulder. Not seeing what was coming seemed worse than seeing it, much as she didn't want to see it either.

And when she did see it, Fiona gasped, stumbling backwards as Inferno took a menacing step forward.

Tinder, her wings bursting from the back of her impeccable gown, slid into the room. She may have flown, Fiona couldn't be sure. There didn't seem like enough space for her to glide around, but Fiona also didn't see Tinder's feet touching the ground. The scales on her face, and the bright redness of her eyes, made her look more like a demon than a dragon.

Seeing a full-fledged dragon in front of her would have been less terrifying. This was a snarling nightmare with eyes only for her.

The guards ran in behind her, but Tinder flew towards the second room where Fiona and Inferno stood. Her arms reached out, whether for her or Inferno, Fiona couldn't tell, but Inferno made sure that he was the one she made contact with.

Tinder shrieked again, as though strips of skin were being peeled slowly from her body as she struggled to make it around Inferno, clawed fingers reaching out for Fiona, answering the question of just who she was after.

"I hate you! You bitch! You fucking bitch! I hate you!"

Fiona tensed, stunned by the display, and then she was angry. "Well, I hate you, too!"

If Fiona was a better woman, she might have had some more forgiveness, but it was impossible to feel overly forgiving when Tinder was, in that moment, trying to get through Inferno so she could claw out Fiona's eyes.

Tinder was the one who sent those men into her apartment, was the one who pretended to be nice to her after she was the cause for the burn on Fiona's face.

Right. She could go and fuck herself. Fiona didn't care anymore.

Tinder's wings flapped violently behind her, scraping at the ceiling, holding back the guards who attempted to get close with little success. Fiona didn't understand why until she took a step forward and saw for herself what was happening. She'd never seen Tinder in her full dragon form. It was rare to see the female royals in their full dragon shapes even in the magazines, but for Tinder, never.

From the looks of things, her wings were made up of many, perhaps even hundreds, of sharp edges, the sort that were dangerous and thin enough to hold back the guards behind her, and peel strips off the wallpaper.

Inferno, however, remained a solid wall between Tinder and the object of her rage. He stood stoically, as though he barely noticed the damage Tinder inflicted on his face and body with her wings.

"I hate you!" She screamed, this time at Inferno, who hardly looked moved by the show. "I hate you! I hate you!"

Inferno shook her hard, only once, but it seemed to be enough to get Tinder's attention. She stopped, her watery eyes wide as Inferno leaned close. "I know. I am sorry."

Fiona blinked. So did Tinder. She didn't take her eyes away from Inferno. Her body trembled before something seemed to break, as though it took her that long before she was able to have a proper reaction to his words.

And she broke down in his arms, face twisting as her tears fell and wings slumped lifelessly behind her. She leaned against Inferno's chest, weeping, and now Fiona did feel some sense of pity, then annoyance at herself for feeling it. But it wouldn't be banished from her. If anything, Fiona began to feel awkward as she stood there, as though she was the one intruding on a private moment of some kind. As though she was the one who was doing something wrong by standing here as a genuine member of the royal family cried in Inferno's arms.

And Inferno held her against him, stroking her hair, shushing her, soothing her.

And Fiona couldn't blame him for it as Inferno allowed Tinder to cry herself out. When she seemed somewhat calmer again, the guards behind her stepped forward, gently taking her arms, pulling her back.

"No!" Tinder wailed. Inferno stepped with her, keeping close as her wrists were pulled behind her back.

"Don't fight them, Tinder. This is for the best."

"You said you loved me!"

"I still love you, you're my cousin."

Tinder's face twisted with more tears, as though that was the last thing in the world she'd wanted to hear.

Okay, now Fiona did full-blown feel badly for her. It was hard to hate someone who cried like that. At least in the moment. Fiona could save her anger and hatred for later, when there wasn't a crying woman in front of her.

Inferno walked with her and the guards outside of the room, and as Fiona kept her distance, knowing the sight of her might set Tinder off again, she couldn't stay away either.

It was sick.

"I'll come and see you later, Tinder. We'll figure this out."

"Inferno, please!"

Fiona peeked around the corner. Inferno shook his head, the guards surrounding both him and Tinder. Eric stood close by Flare, his eyes stunned, but the rest of him professionally cold.

Ember and Blaze had even managed to get there, both brothers looking massively uncomfortable at the sight of the royal guards leading a member of their family away.

Inferno watched Tinder go, regret in his eyes.

Was it hurting him to see this happen? Fiona couldn't articulate how she felt about that.

Then Inferno turned his gaze back to her, and Fiona was struck dumb under the heat of his stare.

27

———

Fiona tensed as Inferno walked towards her. She didn't want to turn away from him. She didn't want to run even though she wanted to. Maybe he could sense that in her. That she wanted to keep her distance from him, from all of the royals and their guards and their dramatic bullshit.

"Fiona, are you all right? Did she...hurt you?"

Fiona clenched her fists. Her back ached from where she'd landed on it, but she didn't want to admit it. She didn't want to feel weak, facing him right then.

He clenched his teeth together, the look on his face suggesting he didn't know what to say. Inferno reached for her. Fiona stepped back before his hands could touch her. "Don't."

His eyes changed, something hurt, something shocked. Fiona couldn't contain how utterly pissed off she was because he wasn't the one who had anything to feel hurt about.

"Fiona, I'm sorry she hurt you. She won't be able to do that again."

"You know, I could get over what she tried to do to my face. This will heal." Fiona pointed to the redness still there. "But she actually tried to kill me twice. Meanwhile, you're standing with her talking about how much you love her! I guess all that talk of torture was fine, so long as my attempted murderer wasn't *her*."

Inferno took a deep breath. She could see his patience was thinning, and Fiona didn't care.

Blaze and Ember came into the room next, stopping at the sight that met them. Or maybe it was the heated vibe that swirled all around. The two bothers looked at each other, then back at Fiona and Inferno. Ember was the first to speak.

"Inferno, you should be there for her sentencing. Charrling is already demanding we get on with it."

Fiona felt that heat rising up within her, and she couldn't stand it, couldn't contain it. "That bitch probably had something to do with it, too! Are you all serious? You're going to take orders from her?"

Inferno briefly closed his eyes, and when he opened them, they glowed a bright, red-orange, like fire, like his namesake. "No, we do not take orders from Charrling. But this is still her daughter we are talking about and a member of the royal family."

"So they get to try to kill me and you treat them like glass. Perfect." Fiona turned her back to Inferno.

"What are you doing?"

She couldn't look at him. Ember and Blaze were still standing in the doorway, and she didn't want to look at them either. She didn't want the attention, she didn't want the titles, and she didn't want to feel as though she was disappointing anyone either. She hadn't wanted any of this. She didn't want to be one of the only humans in the world that could give Inferno powerful children.

She hadn't asked to be attacked, to meet him, she'd only wanted to be a baker. She wanted to make cakes and cookies and breads and sell them to people. She didn't want the intrigue, she didn't want the attempts on her life, and she didn't want the guilt for not wanting those things.

"You want to leave."

It wasn't a question. He knew what she wanted.

Hearing it out loud, however, made it seem so much harsher than she'd thought.

"I don't want to be a queen." She looked back at him. "I'm tired of people trying to hurt me or kill me. I don't want to risk that anyone else in your family will come after me." She looked at Ember and Blaze. They backed off, apparently deciding this wasn't for them to listen to.

Great, and now she felt guilty for insulting them.

"They would never hurt you."

"I wasn't talking about your brothers, or your sister." She looked back at him. "But how could I know that for sure anyway? I bet you never thought your cousin would be doing that to me."

"To be honest, I supposed Charrling most, but..." He sighed, as though uncomfortable to admit to the next part. He didn't have to say anything. She got it. He couldn't look too closely at Charrling because of her station. Because she was related to him. For so many other reasons she didn't want to give a name to.

Because of his throne, his crown, and expectations were always going to be more important than she was.

"I want to go home." Fiona looked back at him. She held his gaze this time. "You said I wasn't a prisoner here, so let me go home." She didn't look away from him, even when the pain in his eyes increased tenfold.

"You would leave all of this, leave me, to go back to your life?"

"It was my life. You didn't have a right to take me away from it."

"I saved your life."

She broke eye contact for just a moment. Fiona took a breath, then looked back at him. Not even just that, she turned to face him, folding her arms because she didn't know what to do with her hands. "Thank you for that."

Inferno rolled his eyes. "I don't want you to be thankful to me. I would have done it no matter the situation."

"I'm still grateful you did it."

Inferno pressed his lips together. "But you want to leave."

"I want to go home. I want...I want to go back to my life. I never wanted to be an Istavan. I never asked for any of this."

"You don't want me going with you?"

This time, it was a question, as though he wasn't sure of the answer.

Fiona opened her mouth, then shut it again. She didn't know what to say to that. She wanted the man he was when he was alone with her, but not the man who'd just allowed her attacker to be carted off as he told her he loved her.

The silence was terrible, and Inferno took it as his answer. His shoulders relaxed. "I understand."

Fiona shook her head, stepping forward. "No, you don't—"

"Yes, I do."

Fiona stopped.

Inferno breathed deep through his nose. "I made you a promise I knew I would not be able to keep. Even if I gave everything over to Blaze, there's too much...too much everything."

Fiona winced.

"You will have your bakery."

She shook her head. "I don't want anything from you. I just want all of this behind me. I'll earn my bakery on my own."

"Even if you won't have me, I promised it to you. I am going to keep that promise." Inferno rubbed his jaw, and she could feel the tension within him, the raw energy he struggled to contain. "I will set out to finding some property for you. You will have your say as well. The equipment and location will all be your choosing."

It felt too much like he was paying her off, handing her something she'd wanted almost as an apology for upending her life in the first place.

"I will have some proper luggage brought in. Pack all the clothes and makeup and such. If you don't take it, we'll just throw it out."

"Inferno—"

He didn't slam the door on his way out. He closed it softly, but Fiona winced anyway, her body, and heart, suffering the worst pain she'd ever experienced in her life.

28

our Months Later

Fiona had to admit, being the ex-girlfriend of a dragon prince did have its advantages.

Once she learned to ignore the heart-ripping sensation of pain that surged through her chest, that is.

Inferno let her go, as promised, and even more than that, he'd released her back to her home city with a bakery of her own. Not just any bakery, either. When the architect showed Fiona the first set of plans, a huge two-story building, she had to put the brakes on it. And demand they remove all the taglines like _From the Famous YouTube Baker!_

Right, she was definitely not a famous YouTube baker, despite everything she'd tried doing with her channel, and there was no way she would be able to pull in enough revenue to keep something like this open for long.

Fiona shouldn't have taken anything from Inferno, but she wasn't selfless enough to turn down her own bakery.

So she'd told the architect to go smaller, and much more modest.

She ended up with the quaint little bakery of her

dreams; something that was more manageable in size and scope. She had a few employees, and though every single appliance in the building was brand new and definitely outside of any budget Fiona could have saved for on her own, she wasn't stuck with too much guilt over the expenses of the place.

The faint scar on her neck, and the residual redness of her face that never went away was a reminder of what she'd endured over a few short days to earn every last fancy gadget.

The bakery was built fast. Within the month of her leaving, and for the next month after that, many people came, from all across the country, dragon and human alike to taste her cooking.

The cooking that captivated a prince.

That's what the papers had said.

Inferno had managed to keep what really happened out of the papers. She went with the story that she'd gone to the palace for a few days to bake for him, and that he'd been so impressed that he'd gifted her a bakery. As to why the royal wedding was called off, that much was a mystery, but at least no one bothered her about it.

Now, in her third month of business, things were slowing down.

Sort of.

There was now room to walk around in her bakery, and to actually look at the cupcakes, mini pies, and tarts behind her glass counter.

The one thing she hadn't prepared herself for was the paperwork, payroll, bookkeeping, taxes, supply orders, and everything else she needed to do keep this place going. Running her own bakery was harder than she thought it would be, and she was happy to have it, but she definitely didn't get to spend as much time baking in her own bakery as she'd thought she would.

Some nights, the fact that she hadn't earned it herself, that it had been thrust on her, everything new, everything perfect, put a sour taste in her mouth. Which was why, when the doors closed and the last customer and employee left, she found herself in the back going over the books. She wanted to figure out how soon she could keep the place running without Inferno's help.

Which meant she also had to focus on marketing.

There was the very real chance that after the hype died down in a couple of months, all of these customers she was enjoying would get bored and decide not to come back.

Which meant collecting emails, offering stamp cards for discounts to her current customers, and getting the app running for people to use on their phones to replace those cards so she didn't have to buy them.

So much to do. So much to think about. Fiona rubbed her face, closing her eyes.

And she saw Inferno.

Fiona opened her eyes again, looking down at the numbers and projections she'd written down. Even still, she could make out Inferno's eyes. The pain she saw in them that last day they saw each other, as her bags were being packed into the limo for her trip to his private jet.

He'd looked her right in the eyes, his spine stiff. To anyone else, he might have looked cold, as though it was for the best that she was leaving, but she could tell.

Had he not been royalty, had he not been, well, *him*...

Anyone else wouldn't have looked their girlfriend in the eye as they'd left.

He did. Because God forbid he look weak and miserable when there might be someone with a camera hiding in the bushes waiting to take pictures and put them in the tabloids.

Which there had been. The very next day, after Fiona arrived home, she logged onto her computer just to see the headlines.

Human Baker Turns Down Dream Job as Royal Baker.

Now that she was the boss, even though she didn't take shit from anyone else, the stress that came with making sure everything was perfect wasn't the smooth ride she thought it would be.

The bell to the front door rang. Fiona froze. Did she forget to lock it? Or was Kate coming back?

She rolled away from her desk. "Kate? That you?"

No answer, just the sound of heavy footsteps.

She rose from her seat. "Sorry, we're closed."

The swinging back door opened. Fiona's heart swelled hard, equal parts relieved and mortified by the sight of Inferno standing there.

He smiled at her, glanced around her back kitchen, then returned his gaze to her. "Thought I would come in and see how things were going."

Fiona blinked, expecting him to disappear. He didn't, and he looked so out of place in her kitchen. She was still wearing her white uniform and her hair was still up and kind of limp from working all day. She desperately needed a shower, and he looked fresh as a daisy in the suit he wore. He looked as though he was getting ready for a big meeting with some powerful people.

Possibly other government officials?

Or something else?

Inferno averted his gaze, a soft laugh leaving his mouth. "Stop looking at me like that. You are making me nervous."

"*I* make you nervous?"

That was laughable.

He shrugged. "Well, only when you look at me like you think I shouldn't be here."

Fiona nodded. He shouldn't be here, not because he wasn't welcome, but because it didn't make sense.

He didn't fit with what was around him.

"I just wanted to see how you were doing. It's not the same seeing your face in the tabloids."

Fiona swallowed, knowing perfectly well how right he was. She'd seen his face enough on the Internet and in the papers over the last couple of days, and it wasn't even close to the same as seeing his actual face.

If anything, the pictures just made her feel worse. "No, I guess not."

Inferno smiled that same, watered down smile. She'd never seen him look so unsure of anything before. "You've healed up pretty nice."

Fiona touched her face. "Yeah, it's almost all gone."

"You look good. Real good."

Warmth flooded into her belly. "Thank you."

That was all she said? She wanted to say more, she thought she would, but Fiona's brain blanked out on her and clicked the light off to take a nap.

Like the total traitor that it was.

Fuck. Say something. She had to say something. There had to be something else she could get out of her mouth, but nothing was coming, and she was just standing there.

In front of *him*.

"Can I ask why you really came here?"

Great. Not exactly the most welcoming question in the world.

Inferno exhaled hard, shaking his head. "I came to check up on you."

"Yeah?"

He pressed his lips together. "That's what I told myself."

Hope flickered in her belly when she thought there would be more. "Yeah?"

Inferno rubbed at his jaw, then shook his head, as though he'd been fooling himself this entire time. "Yeah, I came here for more than a check-up."

He moved before she could react. That was fine, because in the next instant, Fiona was in his arms, pressed to the solid heat of his body, his mouth on hers.

It was less of a kiss and more of a claim, but she didn't enjoy it any less. If anything, her body melted. She was struck dumb with the heat, the thrill of his mouth finally on hers after so long...

Fiona moaned helplessly against him. At night, by herself, she'd thought she could remember so vividly what this felt like. She'd thought she could recreate that sensation using only her mind. No. Not true. This showed her how close to forgetting she'd really been. The intensity was so much sharper than her body remembered, and already she was drunk with it.

Inferno's large fingers threaded through her hair. He pulled out her messy bun. His groan was hard when her hair came down. She felt the vibration of his body all throughout her own.

And then there was his *tongue.*

Warmth pooled down to her sex, and just as Fiona moved her hands to give him a little taste of his own medicine, ready to mess up his perfectly combed, gelled hair, he pulled back from her.

Not just with the kiss, but Inferno stepped away from her. The distance left her feeling suddenly cold. As though she'd just stepped out into a blizzard after sitting next to a warm fire.

"What are you doing?"

Inferno shook his head. "I'm sorry."

"Don't be." She reached out for him. He pulled away from her.

That shock had her yanking her hands back.

"Do you have a reason to be sorry for kissing me?"

Inferno rubbed at his jaw. "Yeah. I do."

Painful needles got her right in the heart from all angles. "Are you engaged again?"

"Not yet, but it's in the works."

Fiona swallowed. "One of the human families?" She didn't want to ask which one.

Inferno didn't specify either. "Yeah."

Fiona pressed her lips together. "I didn't read anything like that in the papers."

She'd seen nothing suggesting Inferno had found someone else to marry at all. He hadn't so much as appeared in public with any woman that Fiona had seen, so there was no chance for the gossip rags to make any speculations about that sort of thing.

Fiona's throat started to close. She fought against it, but that seemed to make it worse. "Are you going to get married?"

Inferno propped his hand onto his hip. "I don't want to."

"Then don't."

"You know it doesn't work that way."

Fiona snapped her mouth shut. She wanted it to work that way; she wanted to argue with him that it *should* work that way. But he was right. It didn't. And no amount of her having a tantrum about it would change that.

"Why are you telling me this?" It hurt too much to know,

and the fact that he'd come this whole way just to tell her made it even worse.

Inferno was silent for a moment, his hands on his hips, his heavy brows furrowed, as if this was the last conversation in the world he wanted to have.

"Well?"

Inferno rubbed at his mouth. "I'm telling you because I still love you. I still want you."

"Because I'm an Istavan?"

He cocked his head slightly. "Did you miss the part where I said I still love you?"

Fiona wanted to laugh. In that moment, she couldn't look at him. "You love me because I'm one of the few humans alive who can give you powerful heirs."

"No, I love you because *I love you.*"

The pain in her chest was alive and clawing at her heart like a monster wanting to eat her alive. "Don't say that."

"It's the truth." He shrugged, moved his hands a little, then put them back onto his hips, as though he didn't know what to do with them. "I wanted you to know that."

Now her heart pounded, but this couldn't mean what he was making it out to mean.

"You sent me away."

"I know. I thought it was what you wanted. That it would be the best for both of us."

Fiona shook her head. "Of course a prince would say something like that. No, forget it, any man at all. Dragon, prince, human or no, you're all just the same, really."

"Fine, if that's what you want to think, then that's perfectly all right. I just want to know one thing."

She looked at him, her arms folded, barely able to contain the adrenaline that struck her.

"Will you take me back?"

Fiona opened her mouth, then shut it.

And then she was angry.

"Take you back? You sent me away."

"I know, you said that."

"Well, you need to be reminded again because *you sent me away*. You didn't even try to make it work."

"I know."

"People were sneaking pictures of me as I left."

"I know. I didn't want that for you."

"Did you ever think that maybe I didn't want to leave?"

"I thought you did!"

His outburst shocked her. Fiona fell back a step, but Inferno didn't stop.

"Everything pointed to that you wanted to be away from all of that. From people who were constantly trying to hurt you. I'd just found out there was someone in my immediate family, someone I trusted, who was trying to kill you, and using actual palace guards to do it. I'm sorry if that threw me for a loop. I didn't want you to die."

Fiona's throat closed. She had to press her lips together because if she so much as tried to say a word, she was going to start crying.

Inferno panted for breath, red scales forming on his face and the backs of his hands. His eyes even changed to look a little more...reptilian. But then, as suddenly as he'd lost control, he regained it. Inferno's composure changed. He straightened, cleared his throat, and his skin suddenly returned to something more normal. "I'm sorry."

Fiona swallowed, barely stopping her voice from breaking. "Yeah, me too."

Inferno wouldn't look at her, and more than anything else, that hurt the worst.

"I should go."

Fiona should say something. She should say anything, but she couldn't. She couldn't get the words to form from her mouth and, even if she could, she wasn't entirely sure what she would end up saying, or if she would regret it.

Inferno sighed, turned his back, and, slamming his hand on the door to her kitchen, let himself out.

She should let him go. He was right. It wouldn't work even if she was supposed to be his one and only. One of the other human royals would be able to give him the heir he wanted. She was sure of it. It shouldn't matter what anyone said about how it worked, and dragon royals had been breeding with other dragons and humans for years. Too many of the human royal families had died out, so it was impossible to keep things nice and tidy the way they wanted to.

Fiona clenched her fingers. The next door she heard was the front door. The little bell chimed as Inferno let himself out.

He would get married to someone else. Some other woman would have his babies, be by his side.

Inferno might forget about her and learn to love his new wife.

But she wouldn't be able to forget him. Not in a million years.

Unable to stop herself, Fiona left her kitchen. "Inferno!"

He was already outside; of course he wouldn't hear her. She ran around the counter and to the door, bursting onto the sidewalk. "Inferno!"

Of course, just as she shouted his name, she had to notice his limo pulling into the lane over, merging with traffic.

No. *No.*

She ran after it, pushing through a couple and narrowly avoiding crashing into a plump woman with her child.

"Sorry!" she shouted as the woman glared at her. "Inferno!"

The limo stopped at the next traffic light. Thank God. She had a chance. She just had to catch the limo. Fiona lifted her hand, waving it. She knew enough about Inferno's life to know the limo would be both bullet proof and sound proofed. So she waved her arm like an idiot.

"Inferno! Stop!"

If he didn't have tinted windows, she might be able to tell if she was making a difference, but she couldn't see a damned thing either. And, of course, like out of a goddamn cartoon, construction workers holding a glass panel started walking away from the back of a van, cutting off the sidewalk she was trying to run on.

"Hey! Watch it, lady!" one of the guys yelled, glaring at her after she barely came to a stop in time to keep from crashing into the glass wall, killing herself.

Sorry, sorry. She watched the limo, noting the traffic light as it turned green. "Could you guys maybe hurry a little?"

More glares from the men holding the glass.

"Bitch, you know we could kill ourselves if we drop this the wrong way? Just wait."

Fiona bit the inside of her cheek. The only reason she didn't crawl under the thing was because, well, she didn't want these guys to drop it on her and slice her in half.

Luckily, traffic was moving slowly in this part of town, even with a green light. Somewhere far up the street there must have been a jam.

"Finally," she sighed, ignoring the glares she got from the construction workers again as she was able to get around them and their glass trap. "Inferno!"

She expected the limo to keep moving straight ahead with the traffic. She didn't expect to see the turn signal start. Oh shit. It was going to move down the faster street. She was going to lose it. Fiona ran faster, pumping her arms and legs harder, waving her arm. "Wait!"

The limo turned, merging with traffic, and was suddenly out of sight around the corner.

Fiona slowed to a stop, panting for breath. Her side hurt. She hadn't realized that until just now. Or how sweaty she was. No. This couldn't be it. This couldn't be the end of it. Fiona stumbled forward a few more steps. Maybe she'd get lucky. Maybe his limo would get stuck at another light.

But now that her adrenaline fizzled, like a pathetic wheeze out of a balloon, she could hardly move another step.

The burn in her eyes, and her heart, was more painful than the day she'd walked out of Inferno's life. This was it? This was how it was going to end for them? With him driving off to marry some other royal human to keep up appearances?

And she realized that her dream of owning her own bakery wasn't enough. She needed more than that.

She needed him.

Inferno rounded the corner of the street, on the sidewalk, his eyes finding hers, locking on.

Fiona stared at him, something light waking up within her. Her eyes burned, but she couldn't stop smiling as Inferno ran across the street. He stepped in front of a few cars. They blared their horns at him, but he barely seemed to notice they were there. His eyes were only on her.

Thank God the traffic was moving slowly. It allowed him to make it safely to the other side of the road.

Fiona ran to him, the blur in her eyes making it difficult

to see him as anything other than a blob in front of her as she crashed into his chest.

And his powerful arms wrapped around her.

Fiona sighed. Those strong, rough fingers pushed her chin up, forcing her to look into his eyes.

"I was hoping you would change your mind."

Fiona wanted to laugh as she blinked away her tears. "I was worried you wouldn't see me."

"How could I not when you were flapping your arms like a chicken for me?"

This time, she did laugh, from the depths of her belly, even as Inferno kissed her.

Fiona was vaguely aware of the people who had stopped around her, taking a look at what was going on now that they recognized one of the dragon princes in their midst. A few cameras flashed, but nothing could pull her from this moment.

Nothing could destroy the happiness bubbling within her.

"Will you have me? For the rest of your life?"

She couldn't stop grinning, tightening her arms around his waist. "You're not going to kidnap me again?"

His grin showed off the whites of his fangs, his voice a promising threat. "I will if you let me."

Fiona thought about it. "All right. Just wait for me to get someone to watch the bakery for the next couple of days. Then you can take me away and propose to me properly."

Inferno nodded, kissing her again. "That I can do."

The End

ABOUT THE AUTHOR

USA Today Bestselling Author Mandy Rosko is a videogame playing, book loving chick. She loves writing paranormal romances that range from light steamy to erotic, and has some contemporary and historical romances as well. You can find her on all sorts of platforms, including Twitch, Patreon, Wattpad, Radish, and more!

Get all the latest news from Mandy by signing up for her newsletter: http://eepurl.com/bQ8HvT

And get the most up-to date information on releases from Eighth Ripple Press by signing up for our newsletter: http://eepurl.com/gcUObH

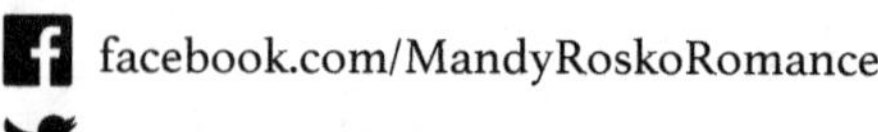

facebook.com/MandyRoskoRomance

twitter.com/rizzorosko

instagram.com/mandyroskodraws

bookbub.com/authors/mandy-rosko

ALSO BY MANDY ROSKO

You've Got to be Shifting Me

Zero Fox Given

Howl Always Love You

Can't Bear to Be Without You

Alpha Bites

Alpha

Alpha Bear

Alpha Dragon

Alpha Wolf

Dangerous Creatures

Burns Like Fire

A Shock to Your System

As Cold as Ice

Gonna Make You Howl

Things in The Night

The Vampire's Curse

The Legend of the Werewolf

The Shepard's Agony

The Dragon and The Wolf

Stand-alone titles

Bad Boy Bear

The Wild Wolf's Wife

Vampires Don't Share with Dragons

Dangerous Guardian

Mate of a Dragon Villain

My Angel Lover Have Mercy on Me (M/M)

Bad Boy Billionaire Brothers

Arrangement with a Billionaire

Holiday with a Billionaire

The Billionaire's Fantasy

Learn more at mandyrosko.com